STONE ARCH BOOKS™

Published in 2012
A Capstone Imprint
1710 Roe Crest Drive
North Mankato, MN 56003
www.capstonepub.com

Originally published by DC Comics in the U.S. in single magazine form as Superman Adventures #2.

DC Comics
1700 Broadway, New York, NY 10019
A Warner Bros. Entertainment Company

Printed and bound in China by Nordica.
112013 007892R
1213/CA21302219

Cataloging-in-Publication Data is available at the Library of Congress website:
ISBN: 978-1-4342-4550-2 (library binding)

Summary: Metallo strikes at the Last Son of Krypton through a woman who's been going around Metropolis claiming to be Superman's girlfriend!

STONE ARCH BOOKS

Ashley C. Andersen Zantop *Publisher*
Michael Dahl *Editorial Director*
Donald Lemke & Sean Tulien *Editors*
Heather Kindseth *Creative Director*
Bob Lentz *Designer*
Kathy McColley *Production Specialist*

DC COMICS

Mike McAvennie *Original U.S. Editor*
Bruce Timm *Cover Artist*

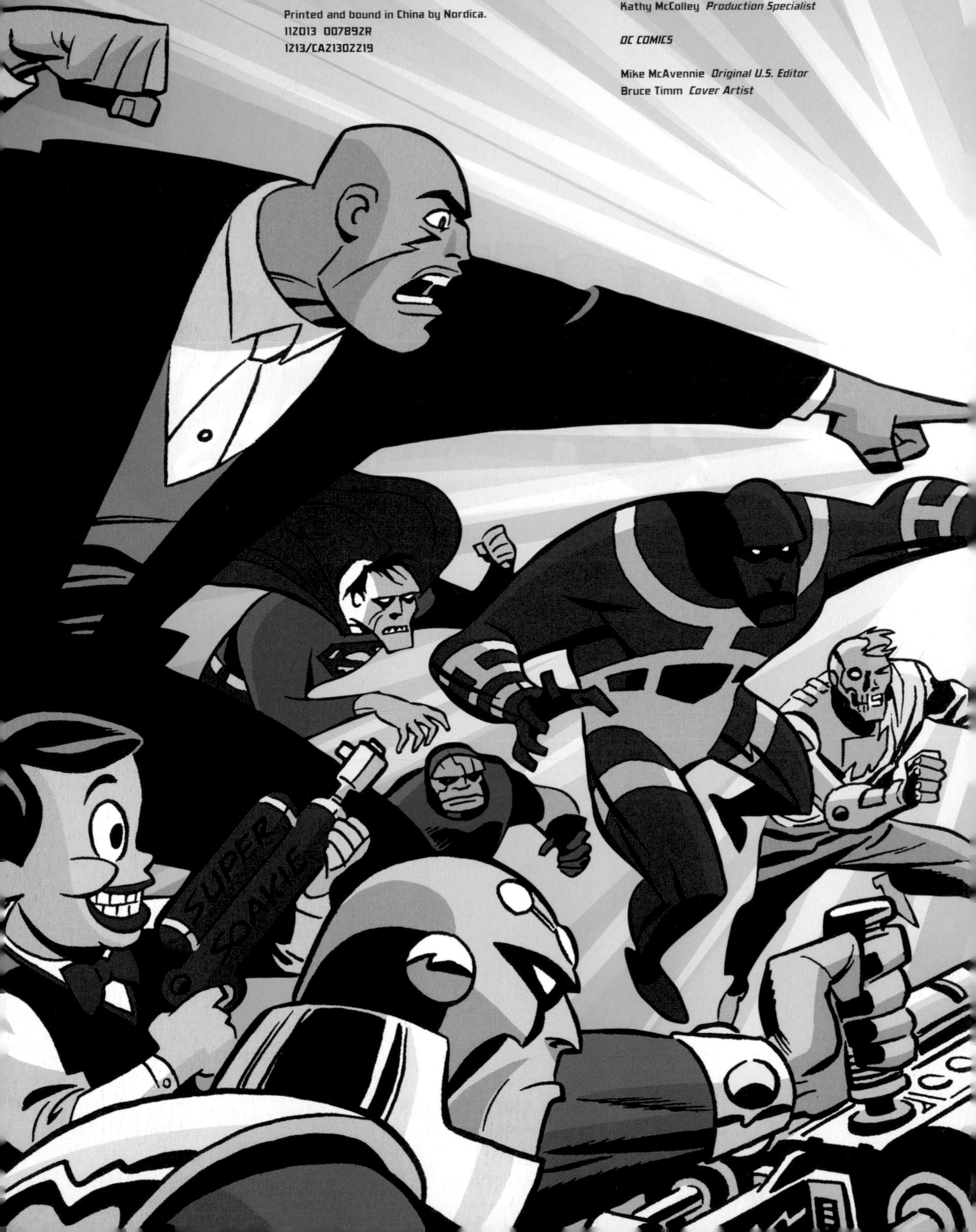
SUPER SOAKIE

SUPERMAN ADVENTURES

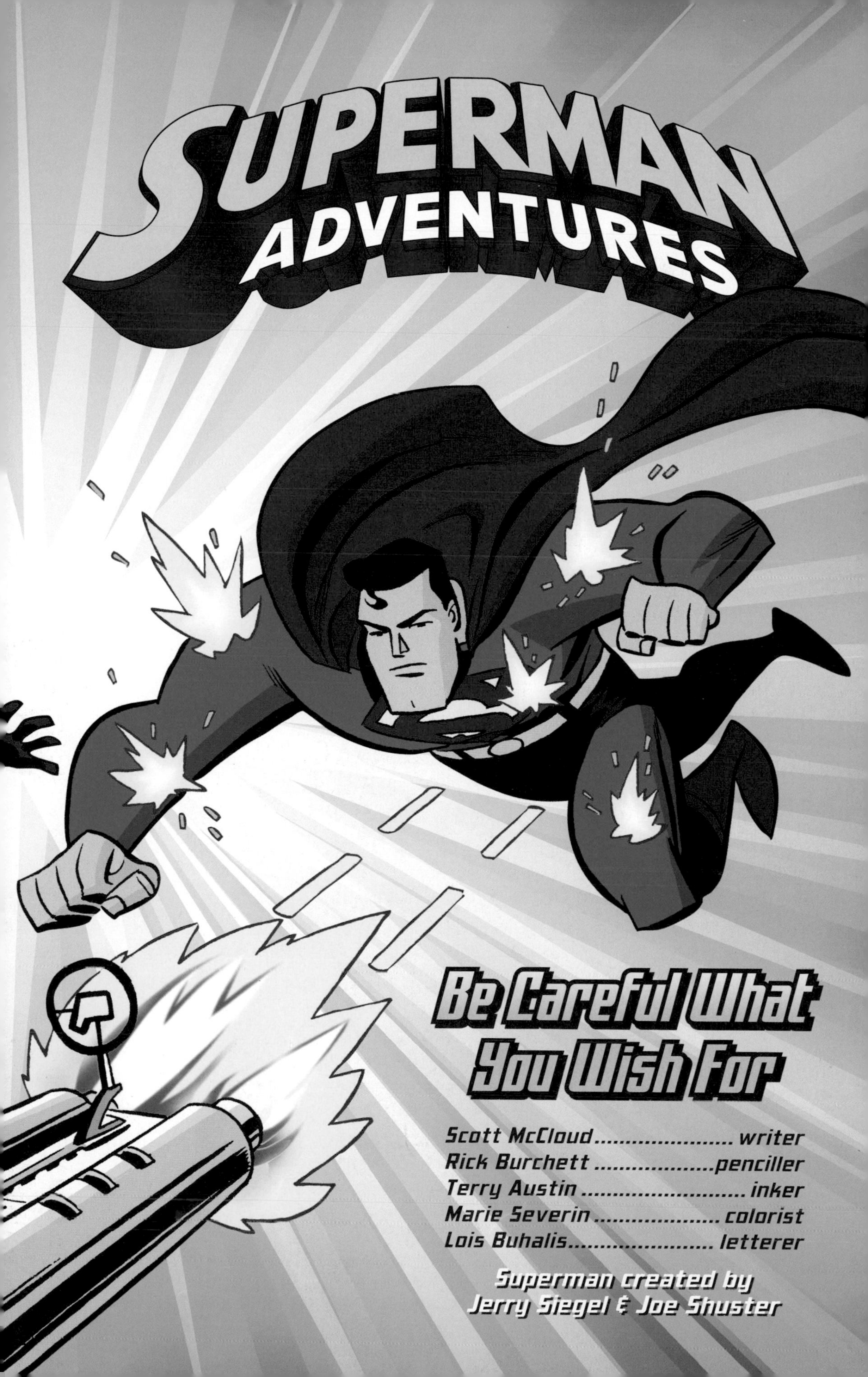

Be Careful What You Wish For

Scott McCloud........................ writer
Rick Burchett ....penciller
Terry Austin .... inker
Marie Severin .... colorist
Lois Buhalis......................... letterer

Superman created by
Jerry Siegel & Joe Shuster

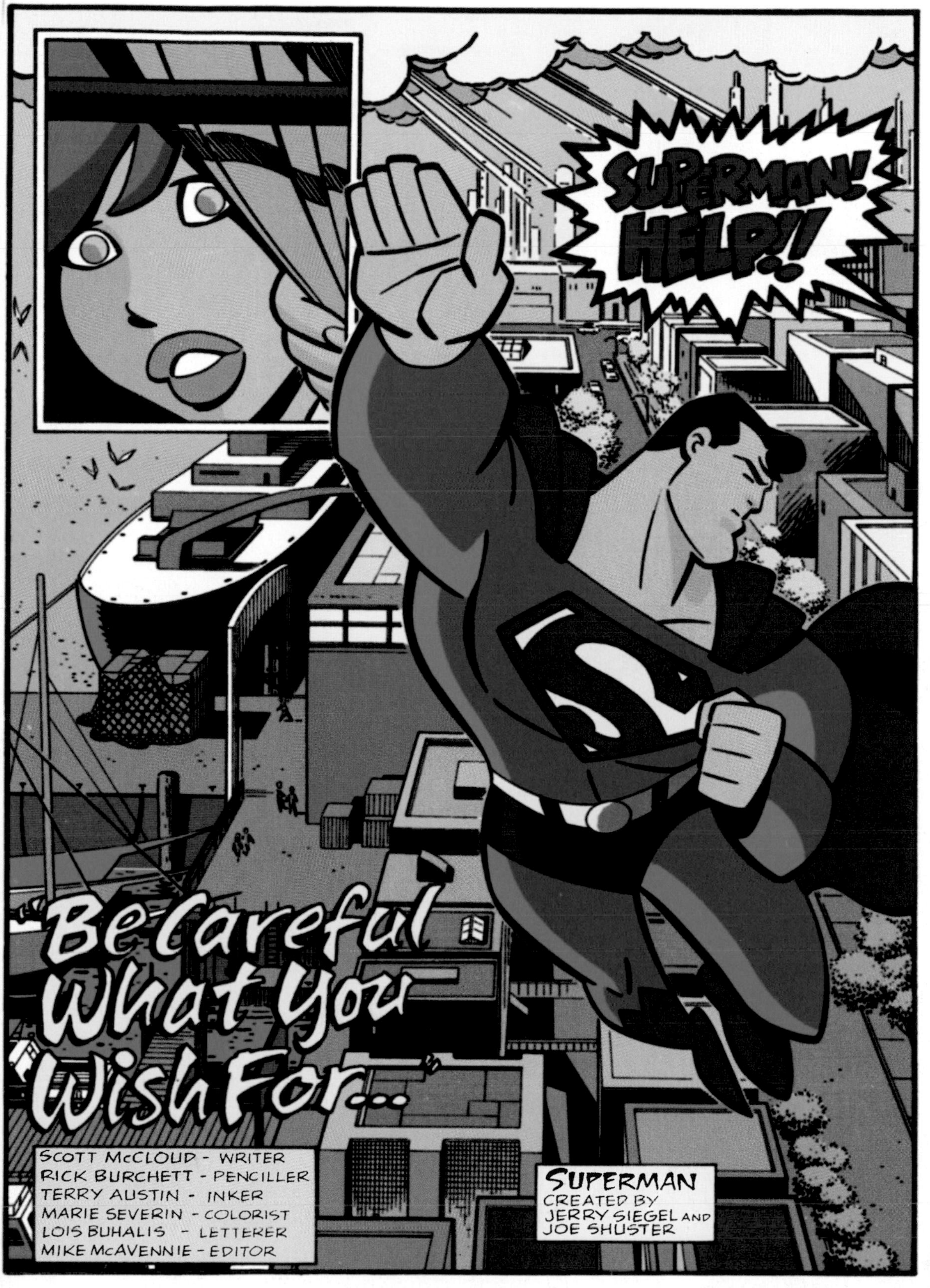
SUPERMAN! HELP!!
"Be Careful What You Wish For..."
SCOTT McCLOUD - WRITER
RICK BURCHETT - PENCILLER
TERRY AUSTIN - INKER
MARIE SEVERIN - COLORIST
LOIS BUHALIS - LETTERER
MIKE McAVENNIE - EDITOR
SUPERMAN CREATED BY JERRY SIEGEL AND JOE SHUSTER

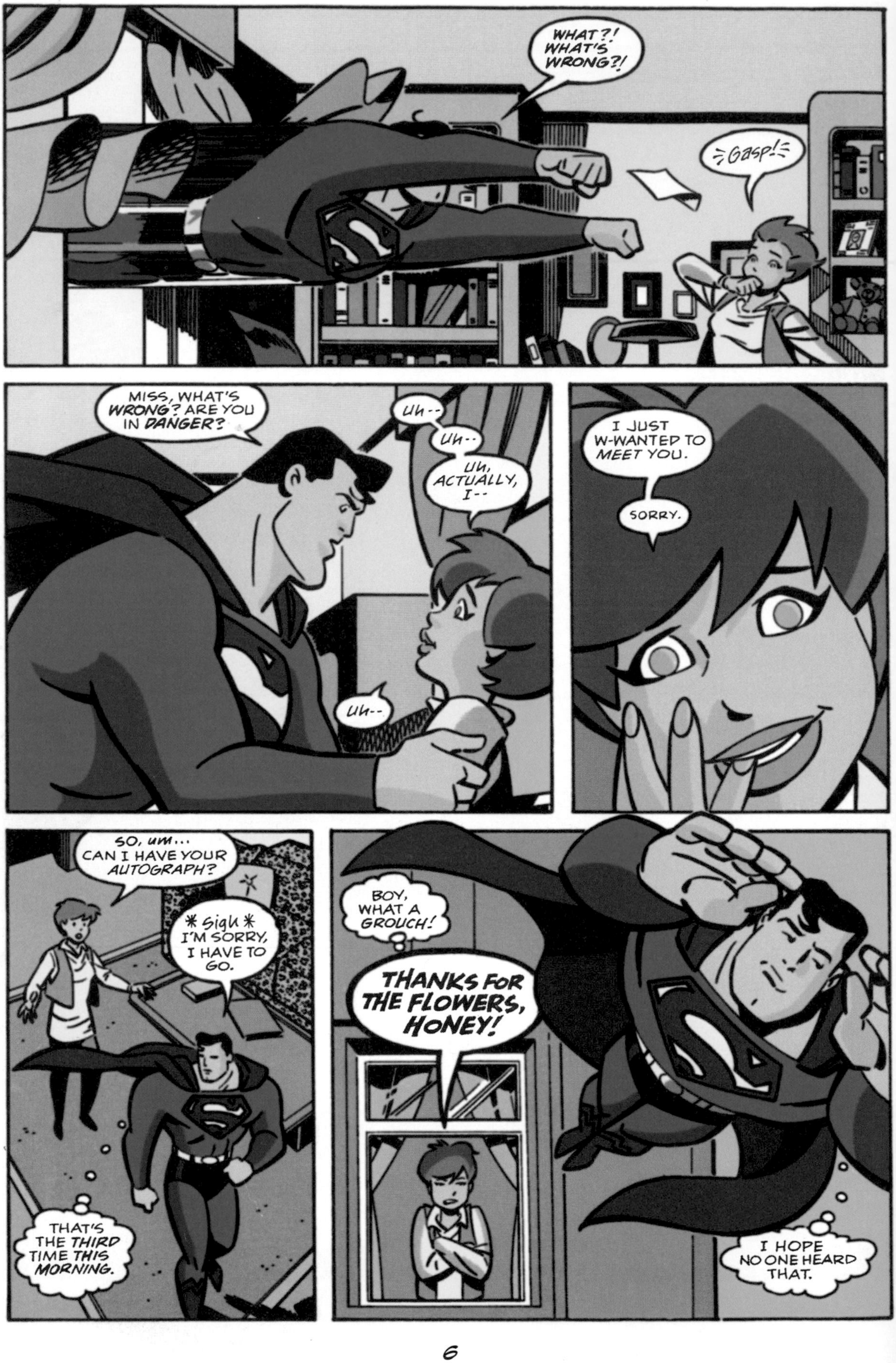
WHAT?! WHAT'S WRONG?!
Gasp!
MISS, WHAT'S WRONG? ARE YOU IN DANGER?
Uh--
Uh--
Uh, ACTUALLY, I--
Uh--
I JUST W-WANTED TO MEET YOU.
SORRY.
SO, um... CAN I HAVE YOUR AUTOGRAPH?
Sigh I'M SORRY, I HAVE TO GO.
THAT'S THE THIRD TIME THIS MORNING.
BOY, WHAT A GROUCH!
THANKS FOR THE FLOWERS, HONEY!
I HOPE NO ONE HEARD THAT.

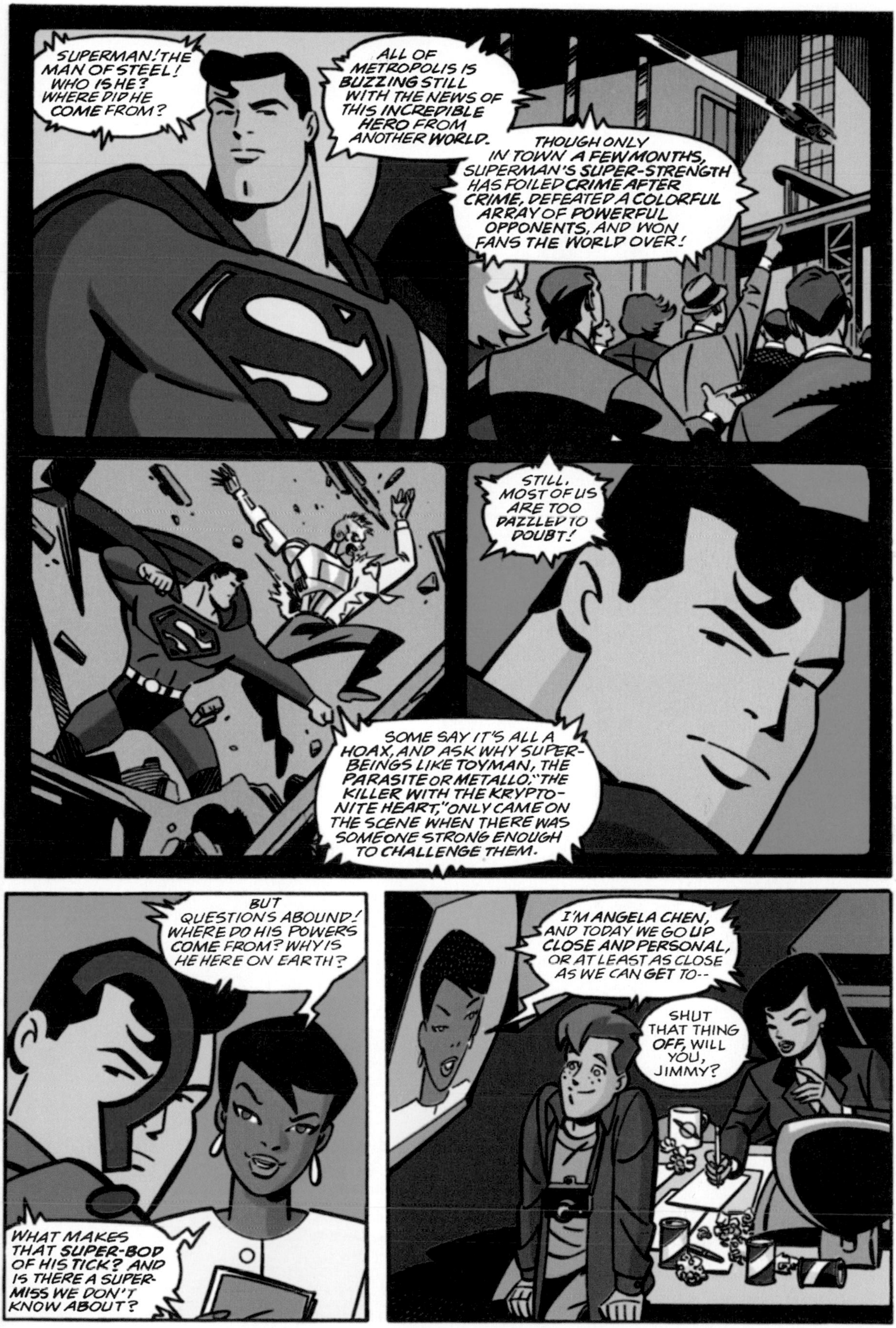

SUPERMAN! THE MAN OF STEEL! WHO IS HE? WHERE DID HE COME FROM?
ALL OF METROPOLIS IS BUZZING STILL WITH THE NEWS OF THIS INCREDIBLE HERO FROM ANOTHER WORLD.
THOUGH ONLY IN TOWN A FEW MONTHS, SUPERMAN'S SUPER-STRENGTH HAS FOILED CRIME AFTER CRIME, DEFEATED A COLORFUL ARRAY OF POWERFUL OPPONENTS, AND WON FANS THE WORLD OVER!
SOME SAY IT'S ALL A HOAX, AND ASK WHY SUPER-BEINGS LIKE TOYMAN, THE PARASITE OR METALLO, "THE KILLER WITH THE KRYPTONITE HEART," ONLY CAME ON THE SCENE WHEN THERE WAS SOMEONE STRONG ENOUGH TO CHALLENGE THEM.
STILL, MOST OF US ARE TOO DAZZLED TO DOUBT!
BUT QUESTIONS ABOUND! WHERE DO HIS POWERS COME FROM? WHY IS HE HERE ON EARTH?
WHAT MAKES THAT SUPER-BOD OF HIS TICK? AND IS THERE A SUPER-MISS WE DON'T KNOW ABOUT?
I'M ANGELA CHEN, AND TODAY WE GO UP CLOSE AND PERSONAL, OR AT LEAST AS CLOSE AS WE CAN GET TO--
SHUT THAT THING OFF, WILL YOU, JIMMY?

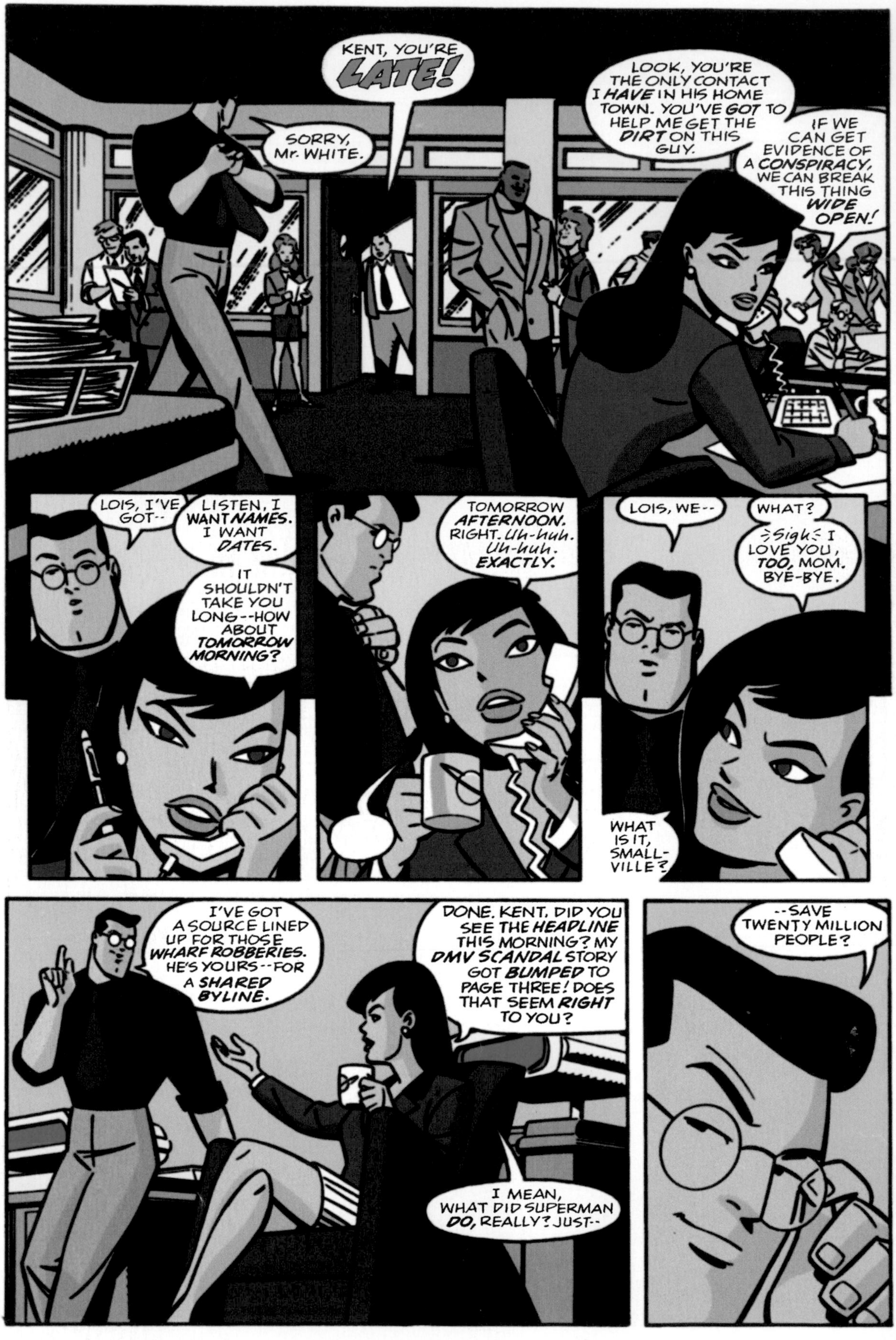

KENT, YOU'RE LATE!
SORRY, Mr. WHITE.
LOOK, YOU'RE THE ONLY CONTACT I HAVE IN HIS HOME TOWN. YOU'VE GOT TO HELP ME GET THE DIRT ON THIS GUY.
IF WE CAN GET EVIDENCE OF A CONSPIRACY, WE CAN BREAK THIS THING WIDE OPEN!
LOIS, I'VE GOT--
LISTEN, I WANT NAMES. I WANT DATES.
IT SHOULDN'T TAKE YOU LONG--HOW ABOUT TOMORROW MORNING?
TOMORROW AFTERNOON. RIGHT. Uh-huh. Uh-huh. EXACTLY.
LOIS, WE--
WHAT?
Sigh I LOVE YOU, TOO, MOM. BYE-BYE.
WHAT IS IT, SMALL-VILLE?
I'VE GOT A SOURCE LINED UP FOR THOSE WHARF ROBBERIES. HE'S YOURS--FOR A SHARED BYLINE.
DONE. KENT, DID YOU SEE THE HEADLINE THIS MORNING? MY DMV SCANDAL STORY GOT BUMPED TO PAGE THREE! DOES THAT SEEM RIGHT TO YOU?
I MEAN, WHAT DID SUPERMAN DO, REALLY? JUST--
--SAVE TWENTY MILLION PEOPLE?

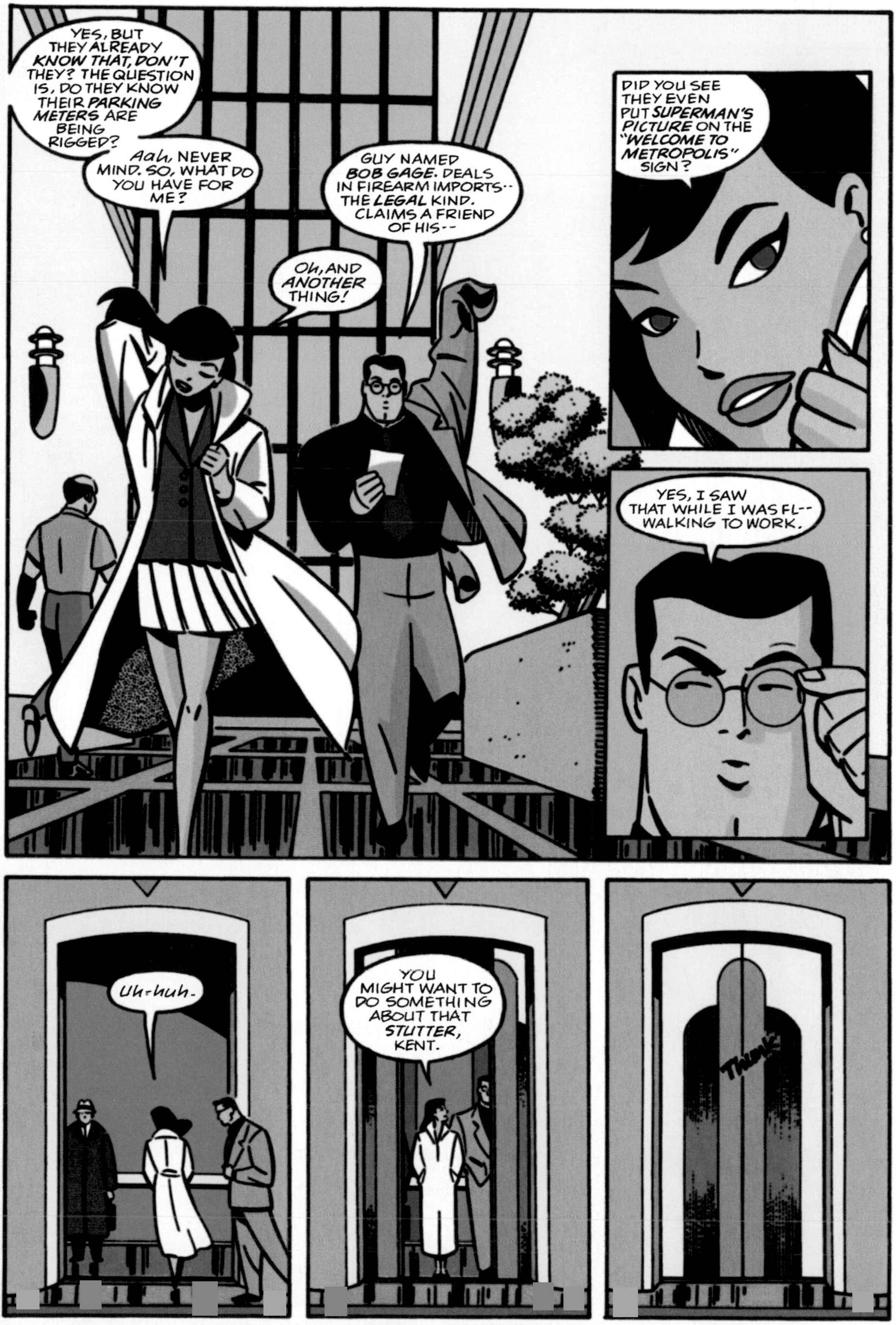
YES, BUT THEY ALREADY KNOW THAT, DON'T THEY? THE QUESTION IS, DO THEY KNOW THEIR PARKING METERS ARE BEING RIGGED?
Aah, NEVER MIND. SO, WHAT DO YOU HAVE FOR ME?
GUY NAMED BOB GAGE. DEALS IN FIREARM IMPORTS-- THE LEGAL KIND. CLAIMS A FRIEND OF HIS--
Oh, AND ANOTHER THING!
DID YOU SEE THEY EVEN PUT SUPERMAN'S PICTURE ON THE "WELCOME TO METROPOLIS" SIGN?
YES, I SAW THAT WHILE I WAS FL-- WALKING TO WORK.
Uh-huh.
YOU MIGHT WANT TO DO SOMETHING ABOUT THAT STUTTER, KENT.
THUNK

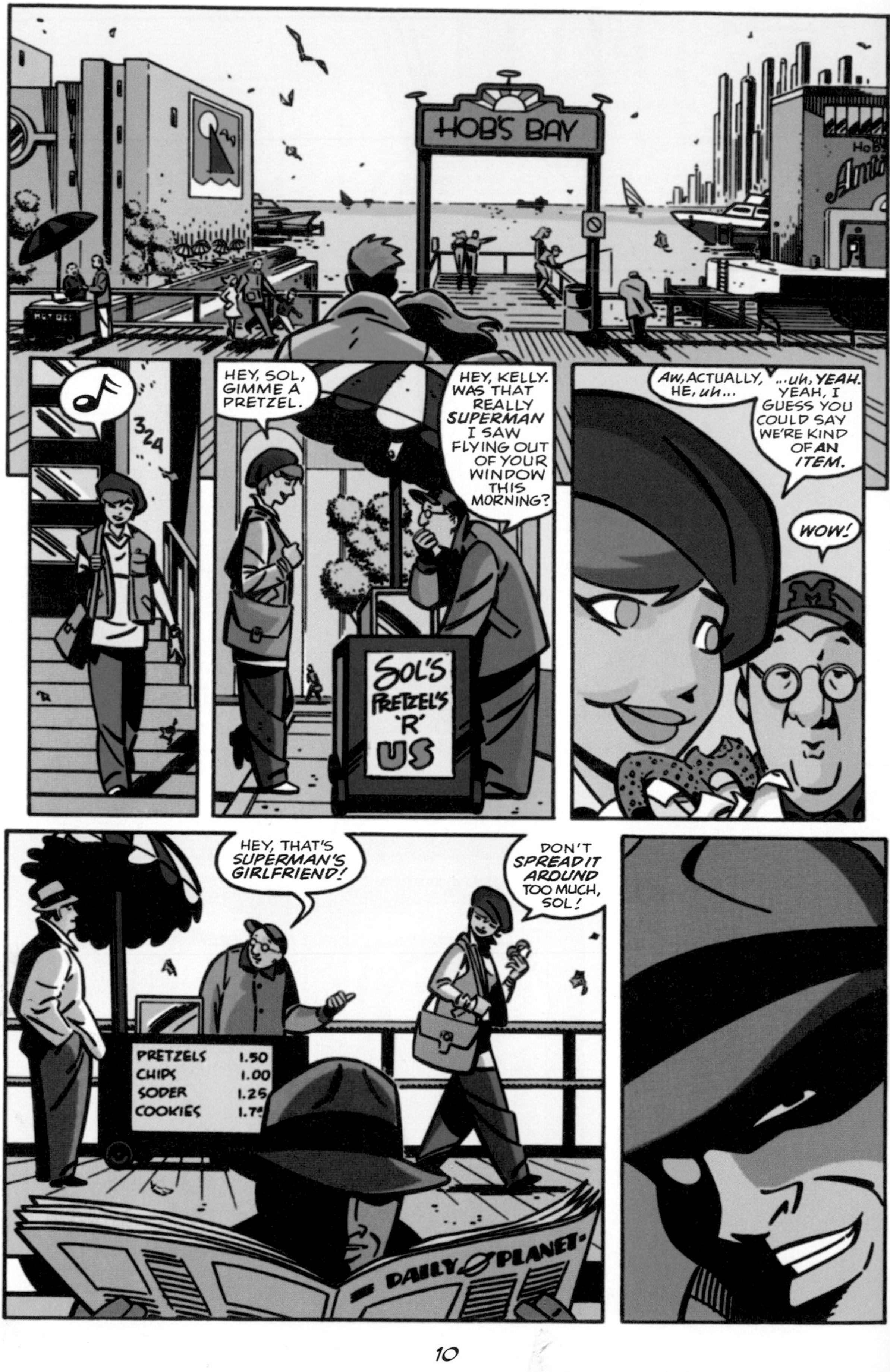

HOB'S BAY
HOT DOGS
♪
324
HEY, SOL, GIMME A PRETZEL.
HEY, KELLY. WAS THAT REALLY SUPERMAN I SAW FLYING OUT OF YOUR WINDOW THIS MORNING?
SOL'S PRETZEL'S 'R' US
AW, ACTUALLY, HE, uh...
...uh, YEAH. YEAH, I GUESS YOU COULD SAY WE'RE KIND OF AN ITEM.
WOW!
HEY, THAT'S SUPERMAN'S GIRLFRIEND!
DON'T SPREAD IT AROUND TOO MUCH, SOL!
PRETZELS 1.50
CHIPS 1.00
SODER 1.25
COOKIES 1.75
DAILY PLANET

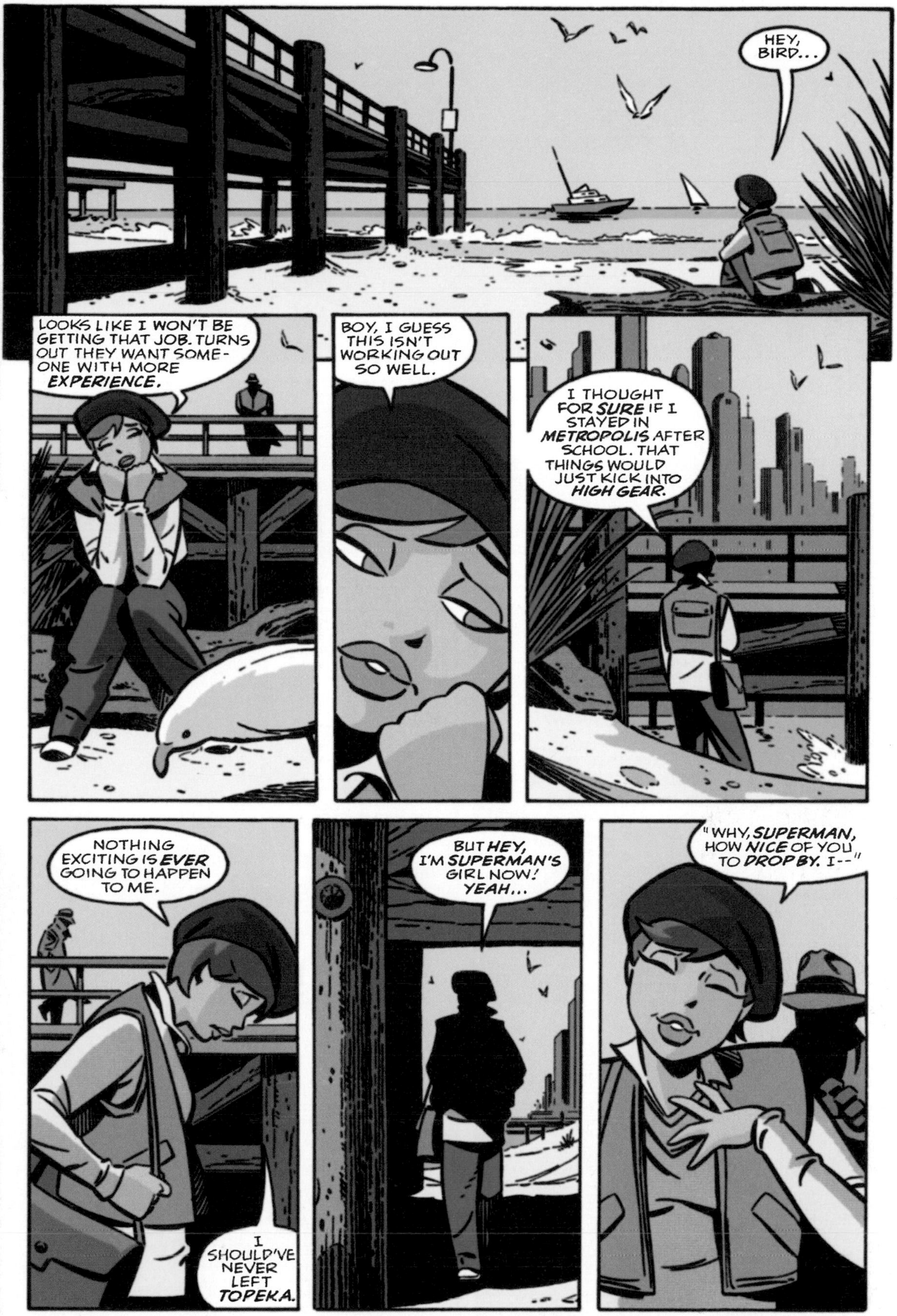
HEY, BIRD...
LOOKS LIKE I WON'T BE GETTING THAT JOB. TURNS OUT THEY WANT SOMEONE WITH MORE EXPERIENCE.
BOY, I GUESS THIS ISN'T WORKING OUT SO WELL.
I THOUGHT FOR SURE IF I STAYED IN METROPOLIS AFTER SCHOOL. THAT THINGS WOULD JUST KICK INTO HIGH GEAR.
NOTHING EXCITING IS EVER GOING TO HAPPEN TO ME.
I SHOULD'VE NEVER LEFT TOPEKA.
BUT HEY, I'M SUPERMAN'S GIRL NOW! YEAH...
"WHY, SUPERMAN, HOW NICE OF YOU TO DROP BY. I--"

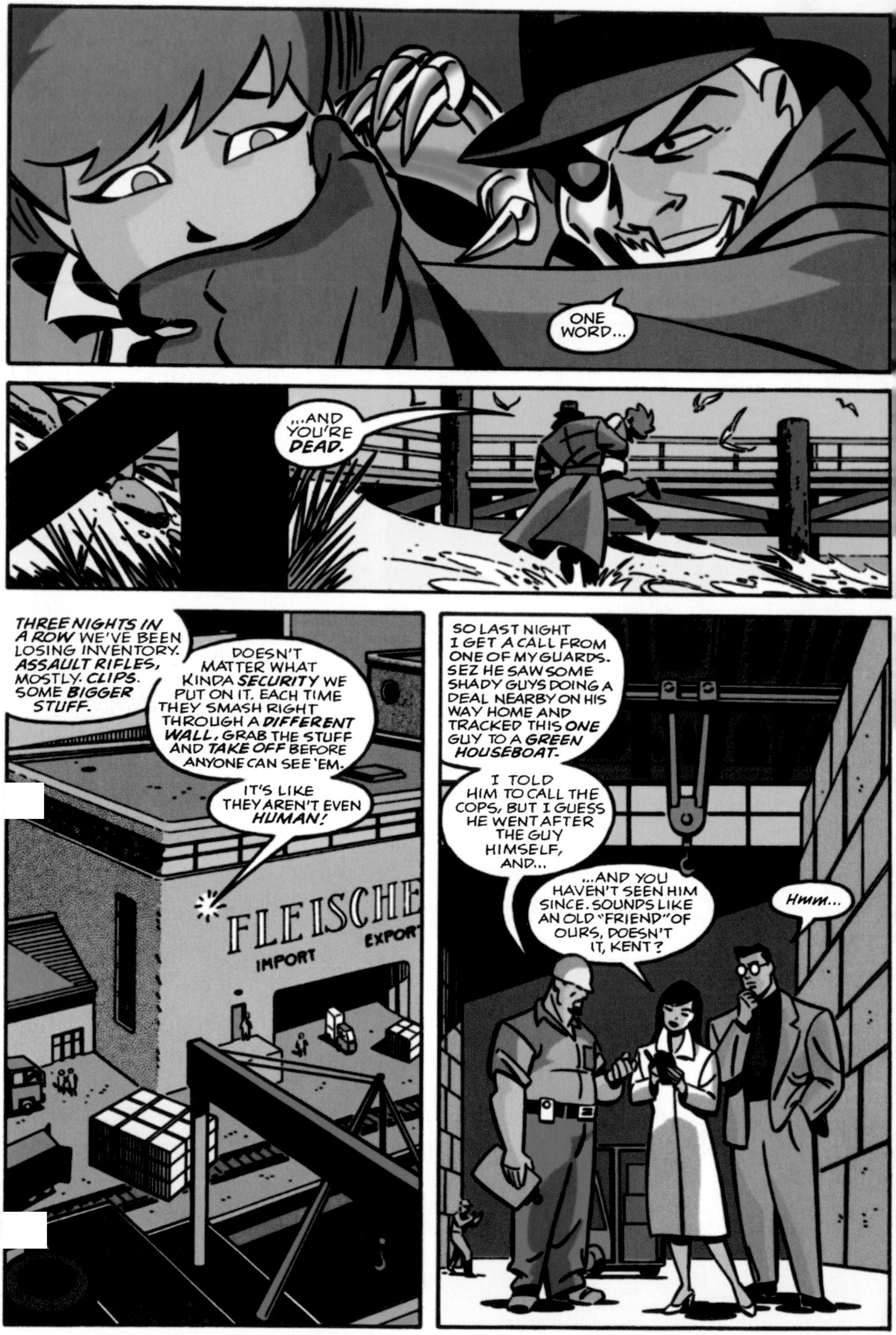
ONE WORD...
...AND YOU'RE DEAD.
THREE NIGHTS IN A ROW WE'VE BEEN LOSING INVENTORY. ASSAULT RIFLES, MOSTLY. CLIPS. SOME BIGGER STUFF.
DOESN'T MATTER WHAT KINDA SECURITY WE PUT ON IT. EACH TIME THEY SMASH RIGHT THROUGH A DIFFERENT WALL, GRAB THE STUFF AND TAKE OFF BEFORE ANYONE CAN SEE 'EM.
IT'S LIKE THEY AREN'T EVEN HUMAN!
FLEISCHE
IMPORT
EXPORT
SO LAST NIGHT I GET A CALL FROM ONE OF MY GUARDS. SEZ HE SAW SOME SHADY GUYS DOING A DEAL NEARBY ON HIS WAY HOME AND TRACKED THIS ONE GUY TO A GREEN HOUSEBOAT.
I TOLD HIM TO CALL THE COPS, BUT I GUESS HE WENT AFTER THE GUY HIMSELF, AND...
...AND YOU HAVEN'T SEEN HIM SINCE. SOUNDS LIKE AN OLD "FRIEND" OF OURS, DOESN'T IT, KENT?
Hmm...

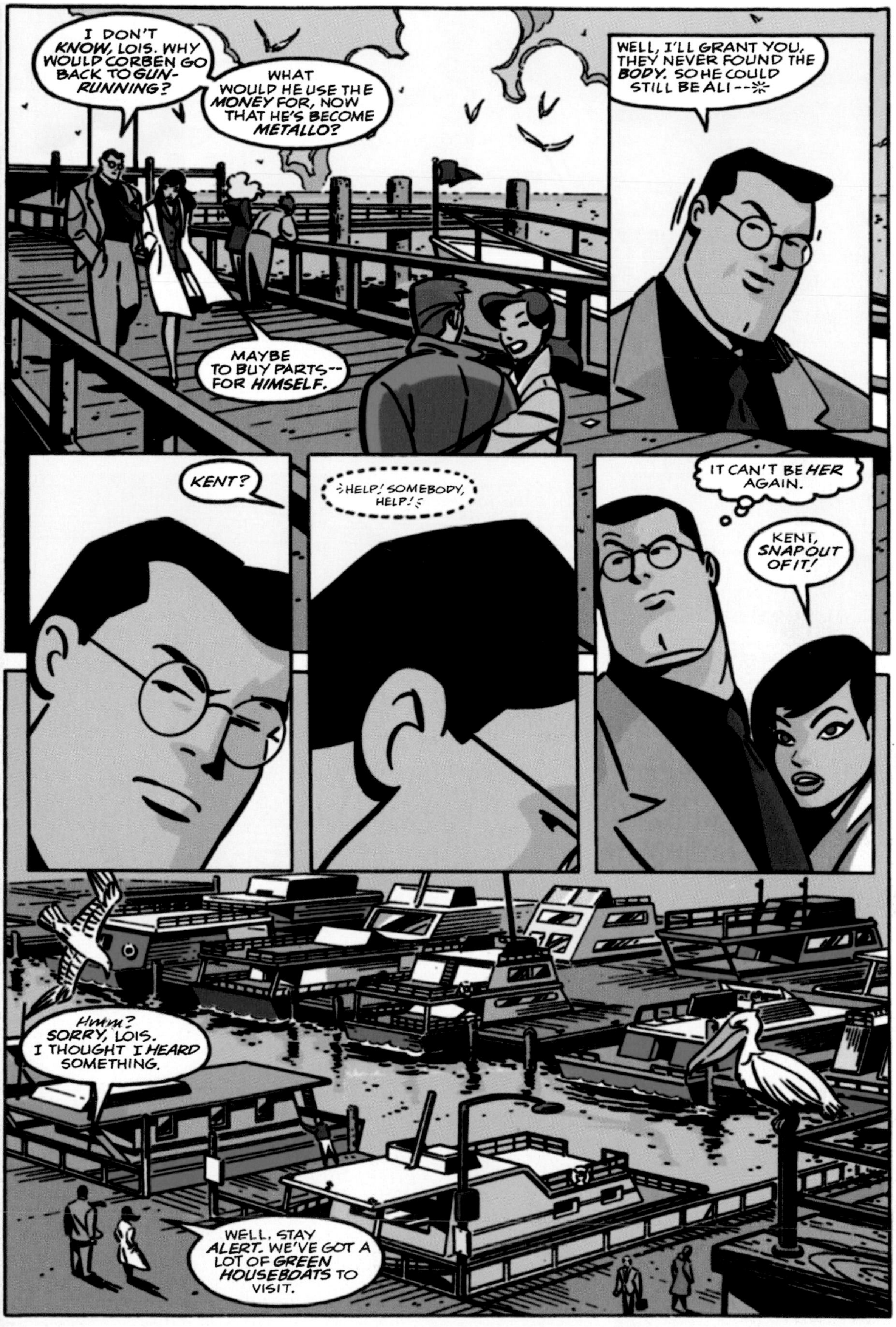
I DON'T KNOW, LOIS. WHY WOULD CORBEN GO BACK TO GUN-RUNNING?
WHAT WOULD HE USE THE MONEY FOR, NOW THAT HE'S BECOME METALLO?
MAYBE TO BUY PARTS-- FOR HIMSELF.
WELL, I'LL GRANT YOU, THEY NEVER FOUND THE BODY. SO HE COULD STILL BE ALI--
KENT?
HELP! SOMEBODY, HELP!
IT CAN'T BE HER AGAIN.
KENT, SNAP OUT OF IT!
Hmm? SORRY, LOIS. I THOUGHT I HEARD SOMETHING.
WELL, STAY ALERT. WE'VE GOT A LOT OF GREEN HOUSEBOATS TO VISIT.

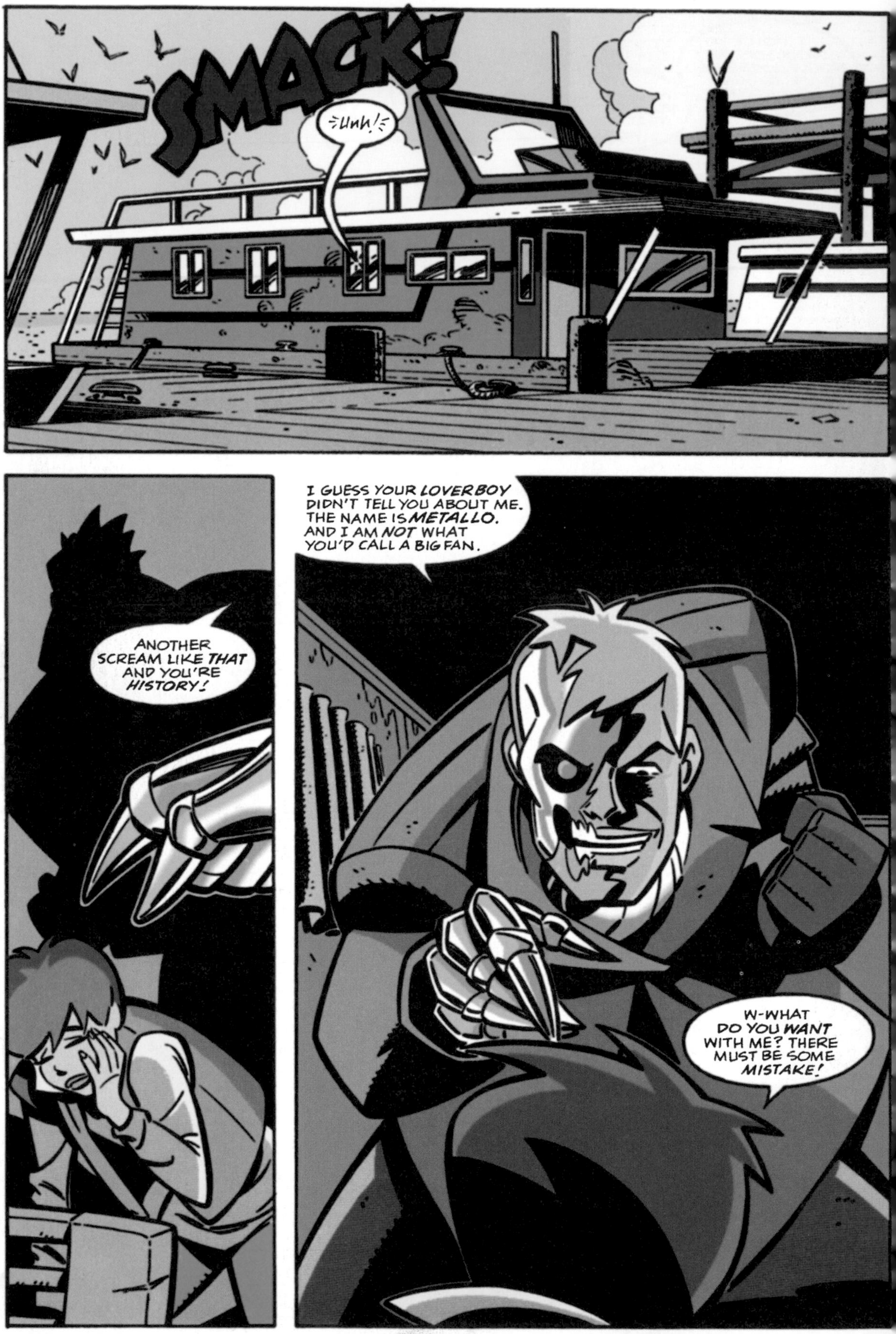
SMACK!
Unh!
ANOTHER SCREAM LIKE THAT AND YOU'RE HISTORY!
I GUESS YOUR LOVERBOY DIDN'T TELL YOU ABOUT ME. THE NAME IS METALLO. AND I AM NOT WHAT YOU'D CALL A BIG FAN.
W-WHAT DO YOU WANT WITH ME? THERE MUST BE SOME MISTAKE!

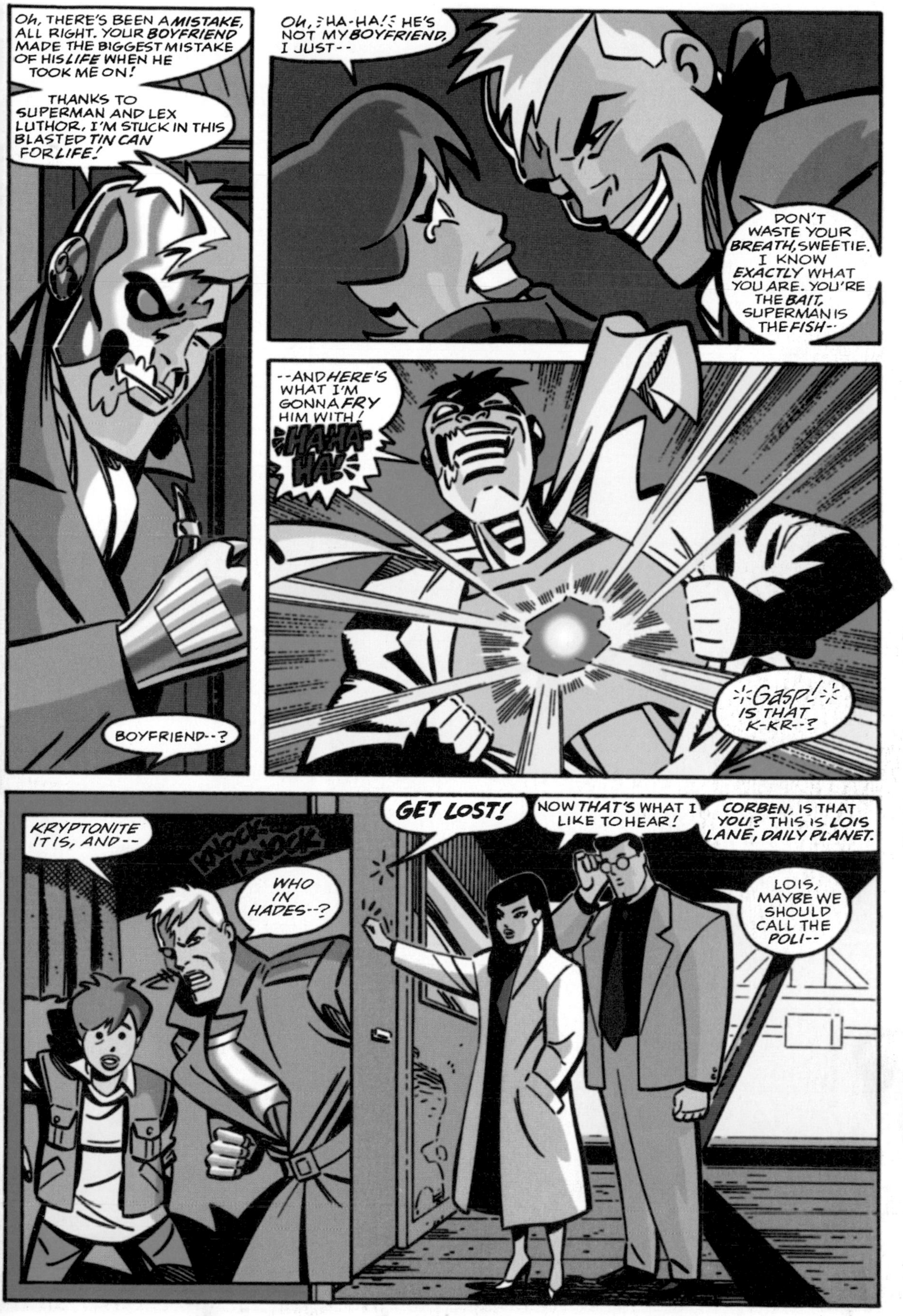
Oh, THERE'S BEEN A MISTAKE, ALL RIGHT. YOUR BOYFRIEND MADE THE BIGGEST MISTAKE OF HIS LIFE WHEN HE TOOK ME ON!
THANKS TO SUPERMAN AND LEX LUTHOR, I'M STUCK IN THIS BLASTED TIN CAN FOR LIFE!
BOYFRIEND--?
Oh, HA-HA! HE'S NOT MY BOYFRIEND, I JUST--
DON'T WASTE YOUR BREATH, SWEETIE. I KNOW EXACTLY WHAT YOU ARE. YOU'RE THE BAIT, SUPERMAN IS THE FISH--
--AND HERE'S WHAT I'M GONNA FRY HIM WITH!
HA HA HA!
Gasp! IS THAT K-KR--?
KRYPTONITE IT IS, AND--
KNOCK KNOCK
WHO IN HADES--?
GET LOST!
NOW THAT'S WHAT I LIKE TO HEAR!
CORBEN, IS THAT YOU? THIS IS LOIS LANE, DAILY PLANET.
LOIS, MAYBE WE SHOULD CALL THE POLI--

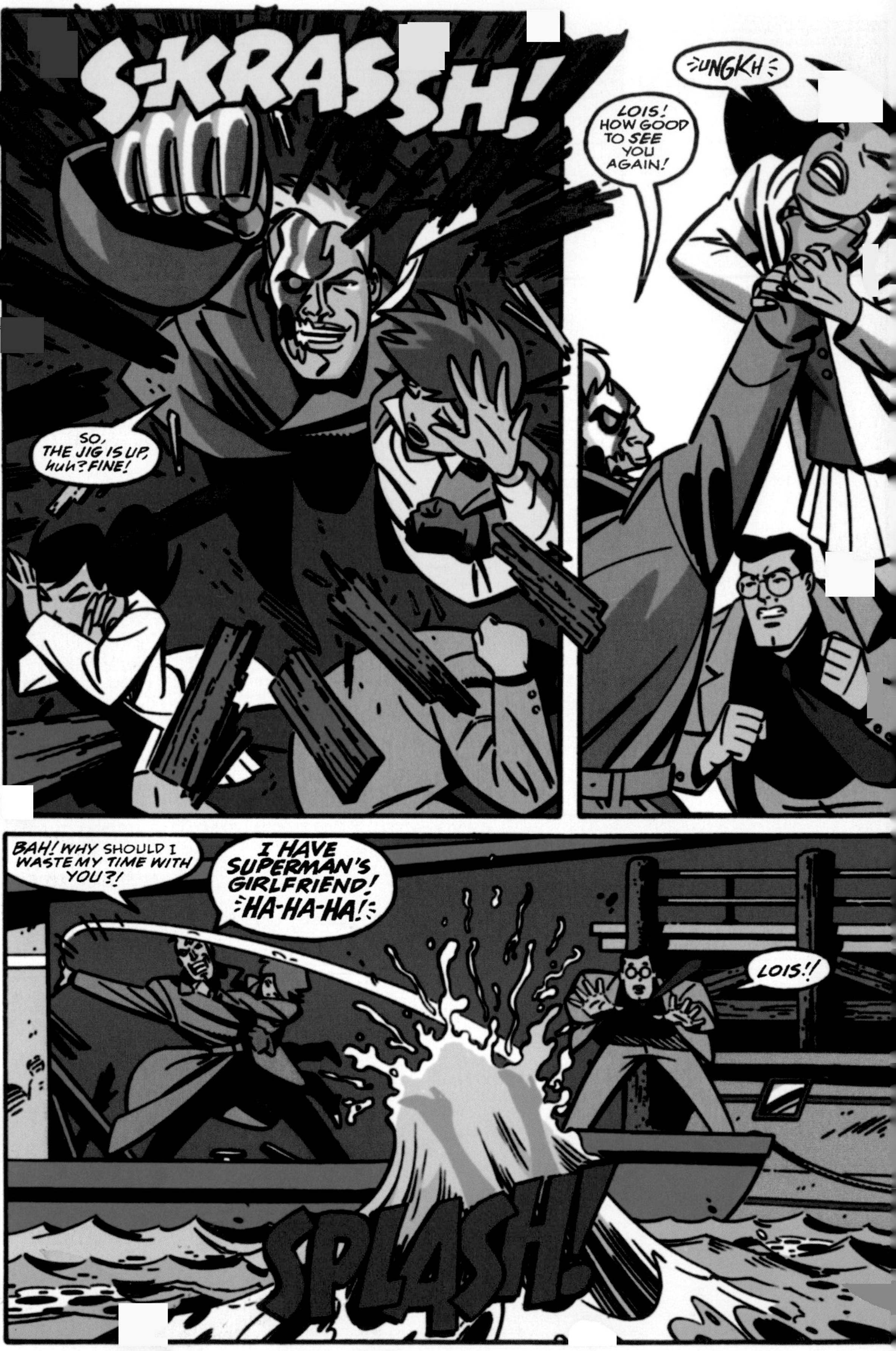
S-KRASSH!
SO, THE JIG IS UP, huh? FINE!
UNGKH
LOIS! HOW GOOD TO SEE YOU AGAIN!
BAH! WHY SHOULD I WASTE MY TIME WITH YOU?!
I HAVE SUPERMAN'S GIRLFRIEND! HA-HA-HA!
LOIS!!
SPLASH!

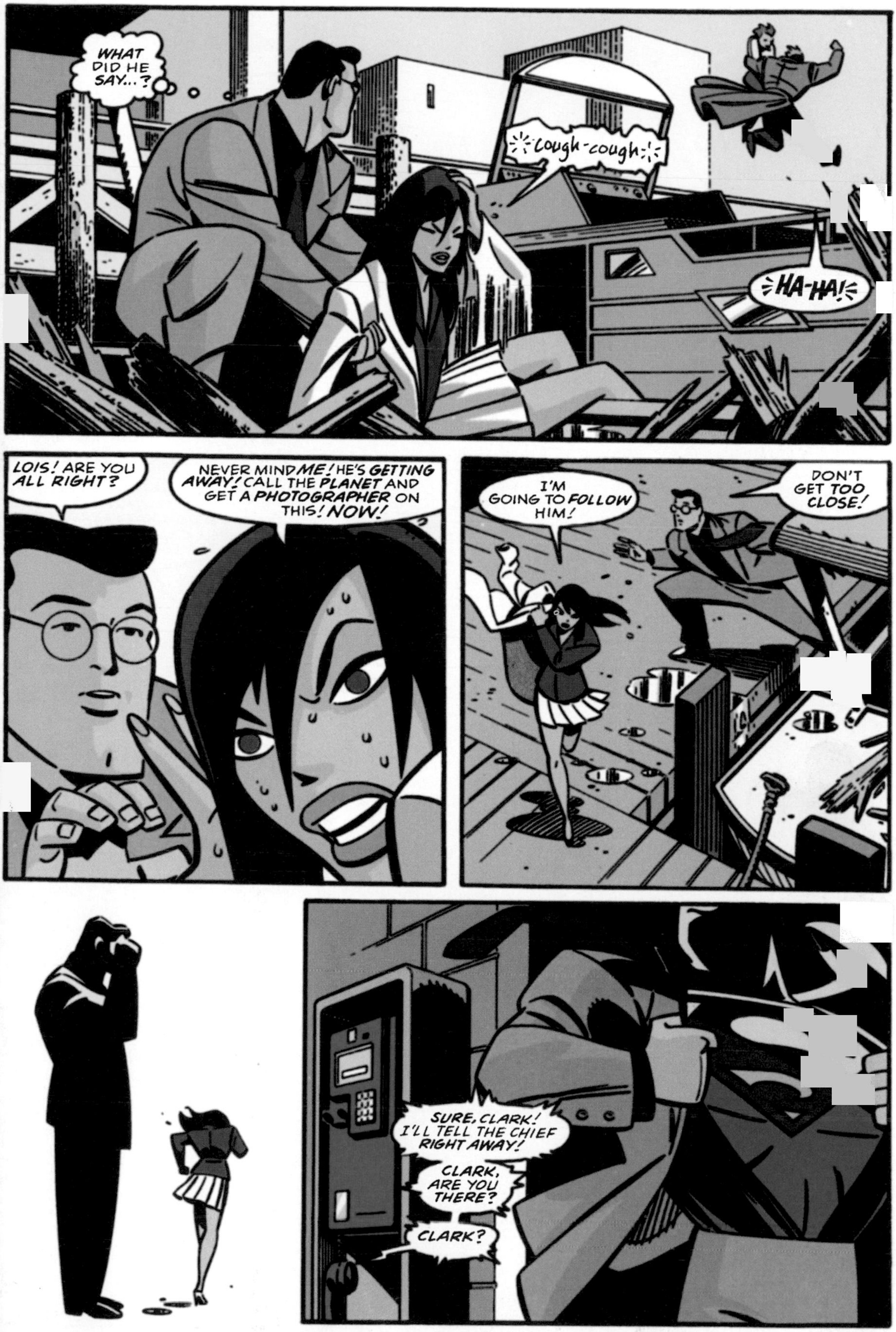
WHAT DID HE SAY...?
COUGH-COUGH
HA-HA!
LOIS! ARE YOU ALL RIGHT?
NEVER MIND ME! HE'S GETTING AWAY! CALL THE PLANET AND GET A PHOTOGRAPHER ON THIS! NOW!
I'M GOING TO FOLLOW HIM!
DON'T GET TOO CLOSE!
SURE, CLARK! I'LL TELL THE CHIEF RIGHT AWAY!
CLARK, ARE YOU THERE?
CLARK?

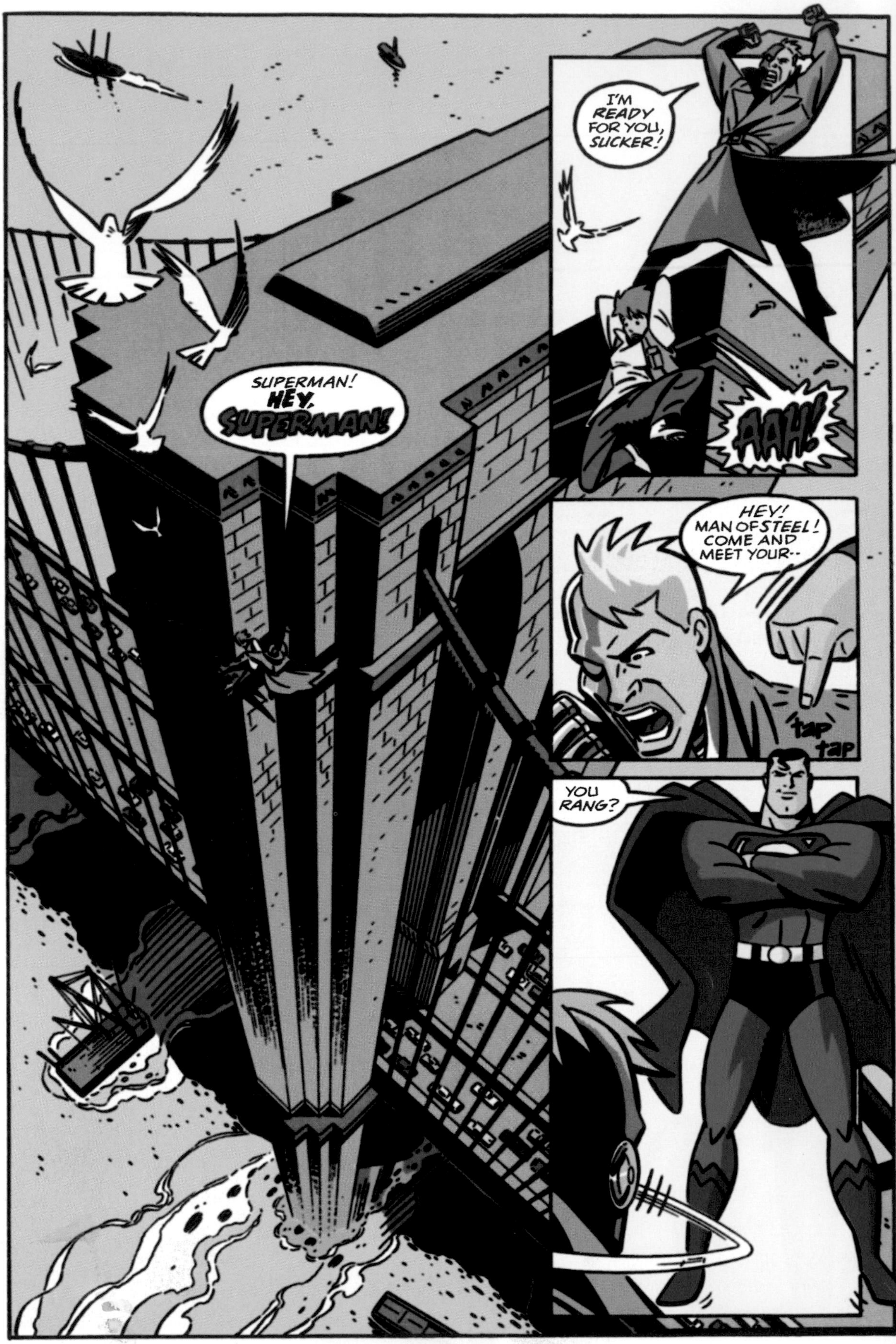
SUPERMAN! HEY, SUPERMAN!
I'M READY FOR YOU, SUCKER!
AAH!
HEY! MAN OF STEEL! COME AND MEET YOUR--
tap tap
YOU RANG?

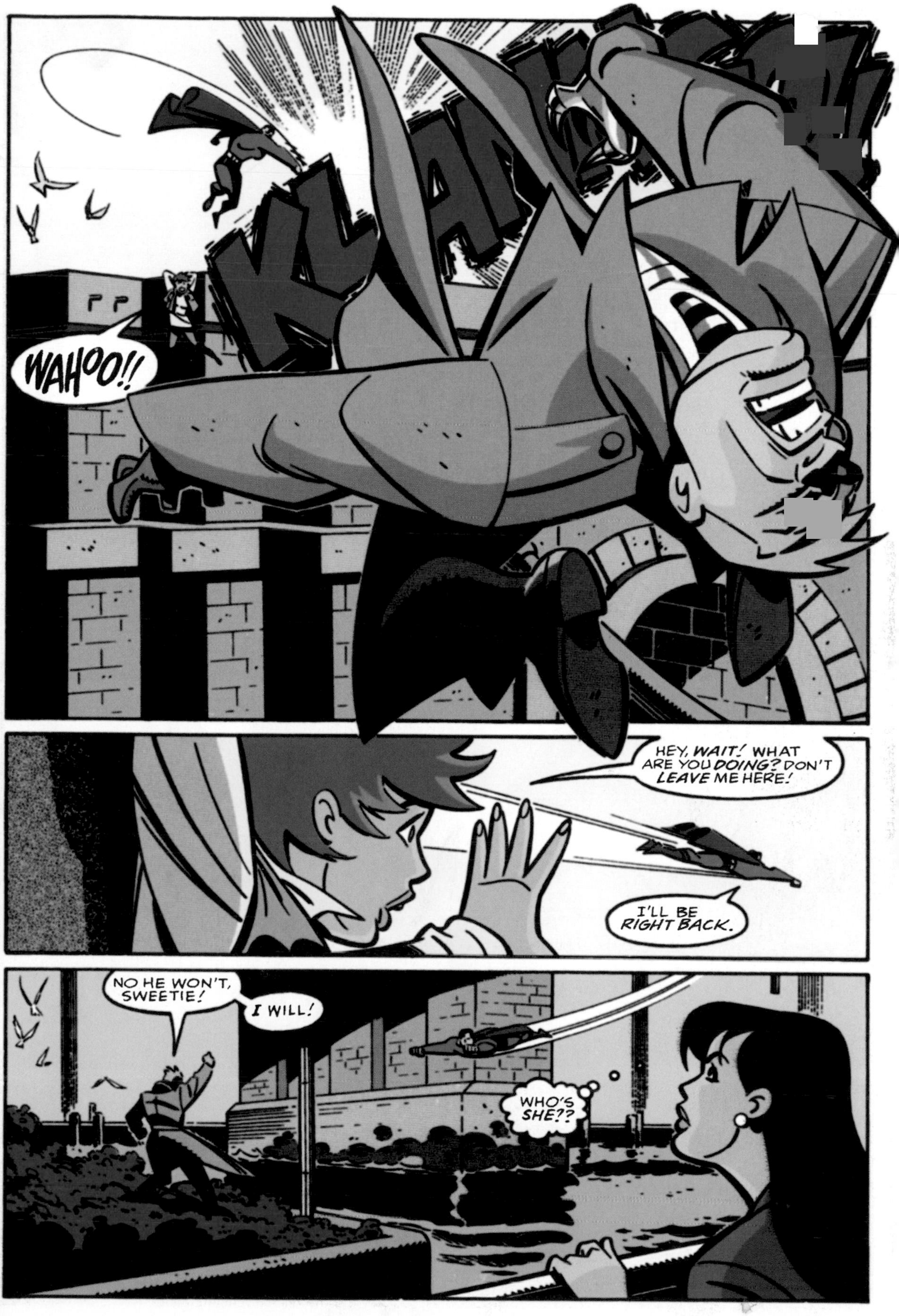
WAHOO!!
HEY, WAIT! WHAT ARE YOU DOING? DON'T LEAVE ME HERE!
I'LL BE RIGHT BACK.
NO HE WON'T, SWEETIE!
I WILL!
WHO'S SHE??

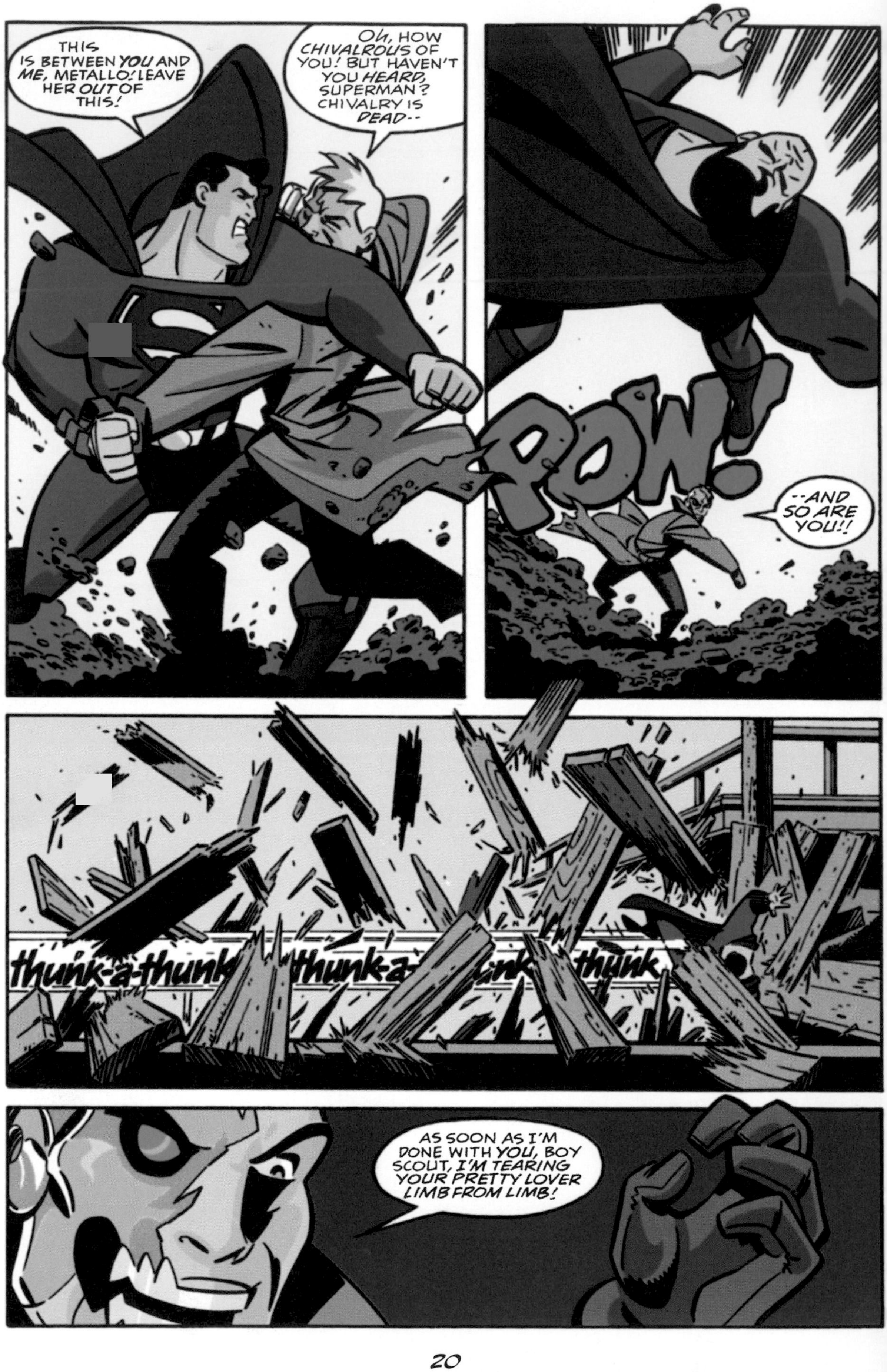
THIS IS BETWEEN YOU AND ME, METALLO! LEAVE HER OUT OF THIS!
OH, HOW CHIVALROUS OF YOU! BUT HAVEN'T YOU HEARD, SUPERMAN? CHIVALRY IS DEAD--
POW!
--AND SO ARE YOU!!
thunk-a-thunk thunk-a- thunk
AS SOON AS I'M DONE WITH YOU, BOY SCOUT, I'M TEARING YOUR PRETTY LOVER LIMB FROM LIMB!

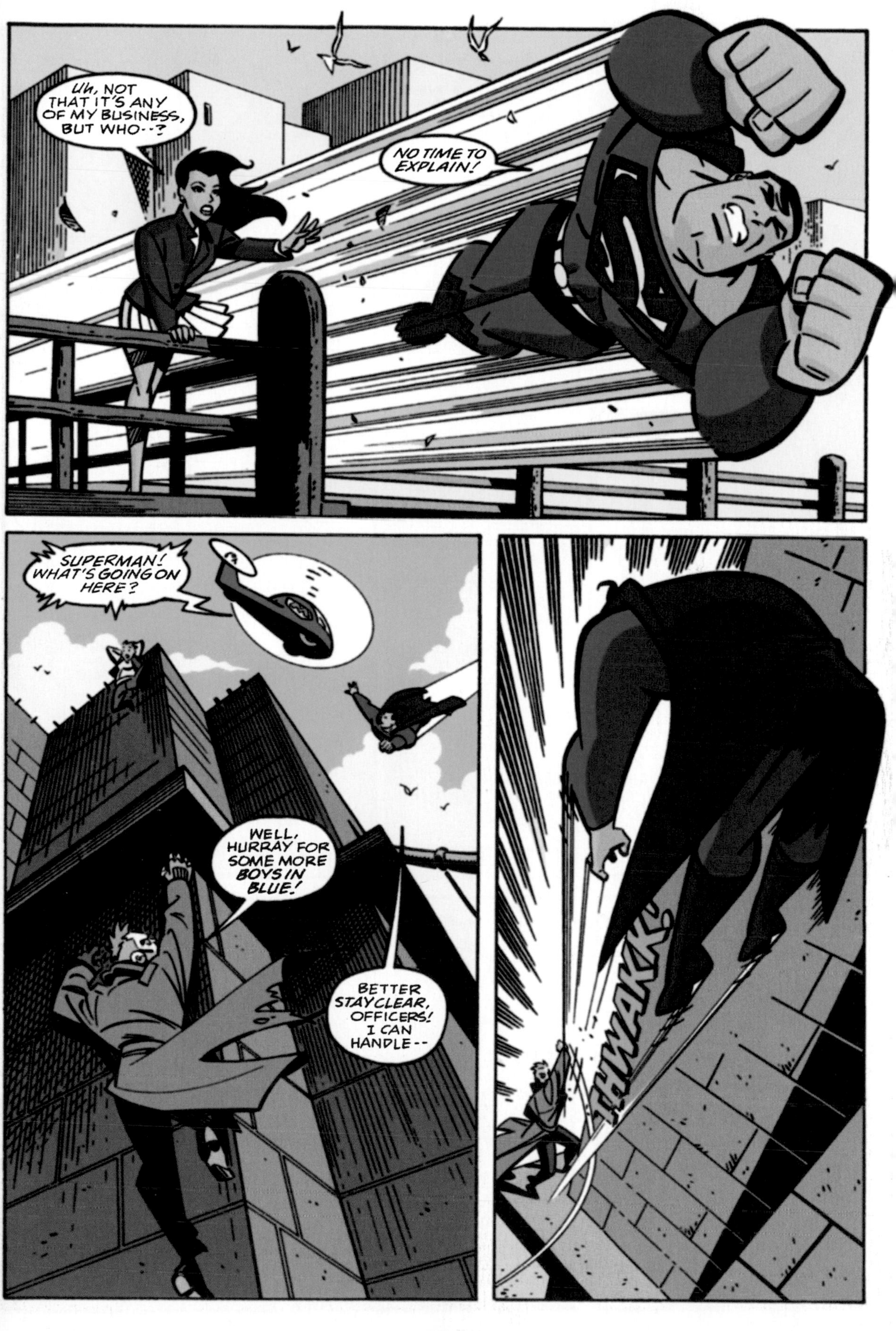

UH, NOT THAT IT'S ANY OF MY BUSINESS, BUT WHO--?
NO TIME TO EXPLAIN!
SUPERMAN! WHAT'S GOING ON HERE?
WELL, HURRAY FOR SOME MORE BOYS IN BLUE!
BETTER STAY CLEAR, OFFICERS! I CAN HANDLE--
THWAKK!

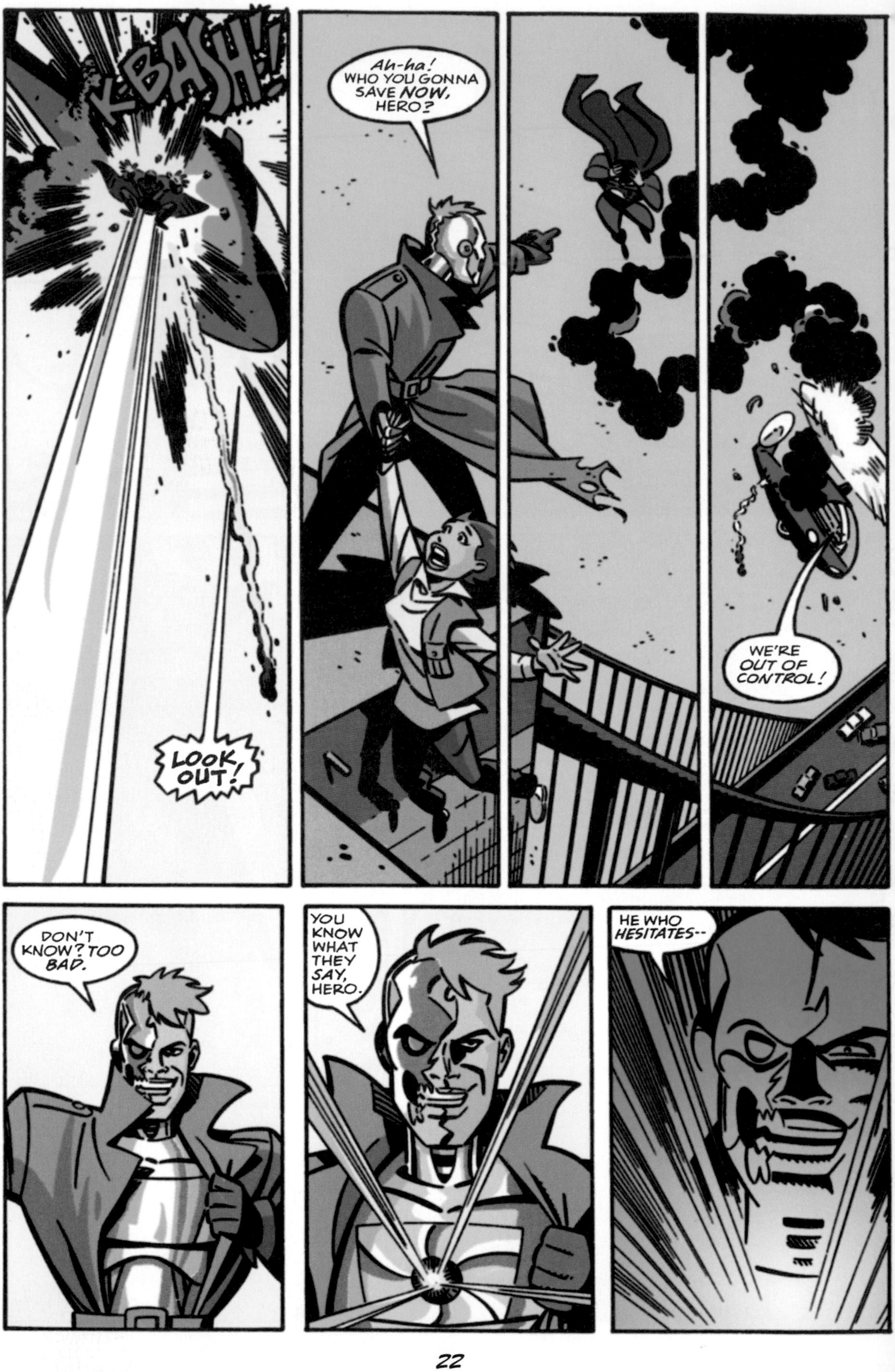
K-BASH!!
LOOK OUT!
Ah-ha! WHO YOU GONNA SAVE NOW, HERO?
WE'RE OUT OF CONTROL!
DON'T KNOW? TOO BAD.
YOU KNOW WHAT THEY SAY, HERO.
HE WHO HESITATES--

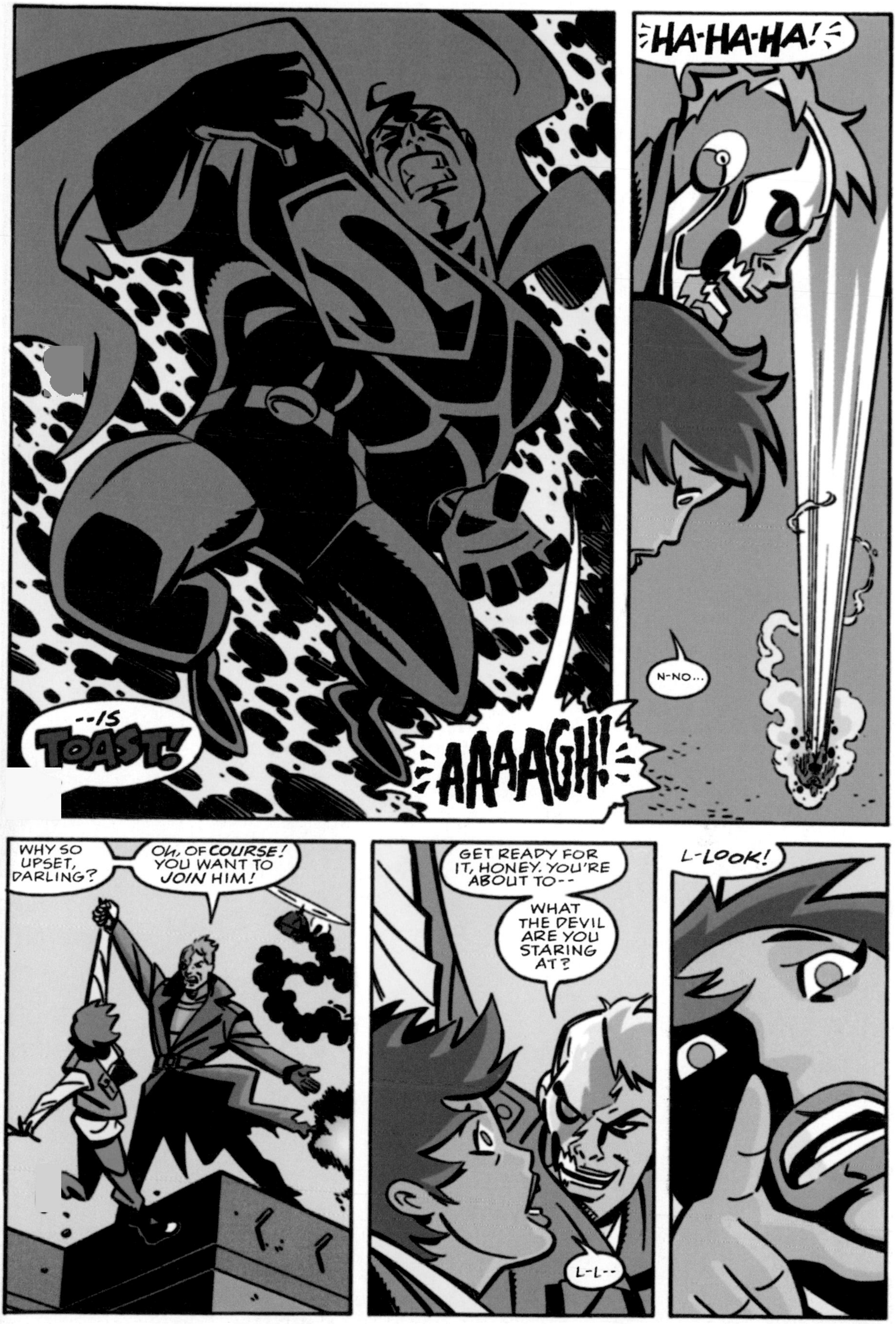

--IS TOAST!
AAAAGH!
HA-HA-HA!
N-NO...
WHY SO UPSET, DARLING?
OH, OF COURSE! YOU WANT TO JOIN HIM!
GET READY FOR IT, HONEY. YOU'RE ABOUT TO--
WHAT THE DEVIL ARE YOU STARING AT?
L-L--
L-LOOK!

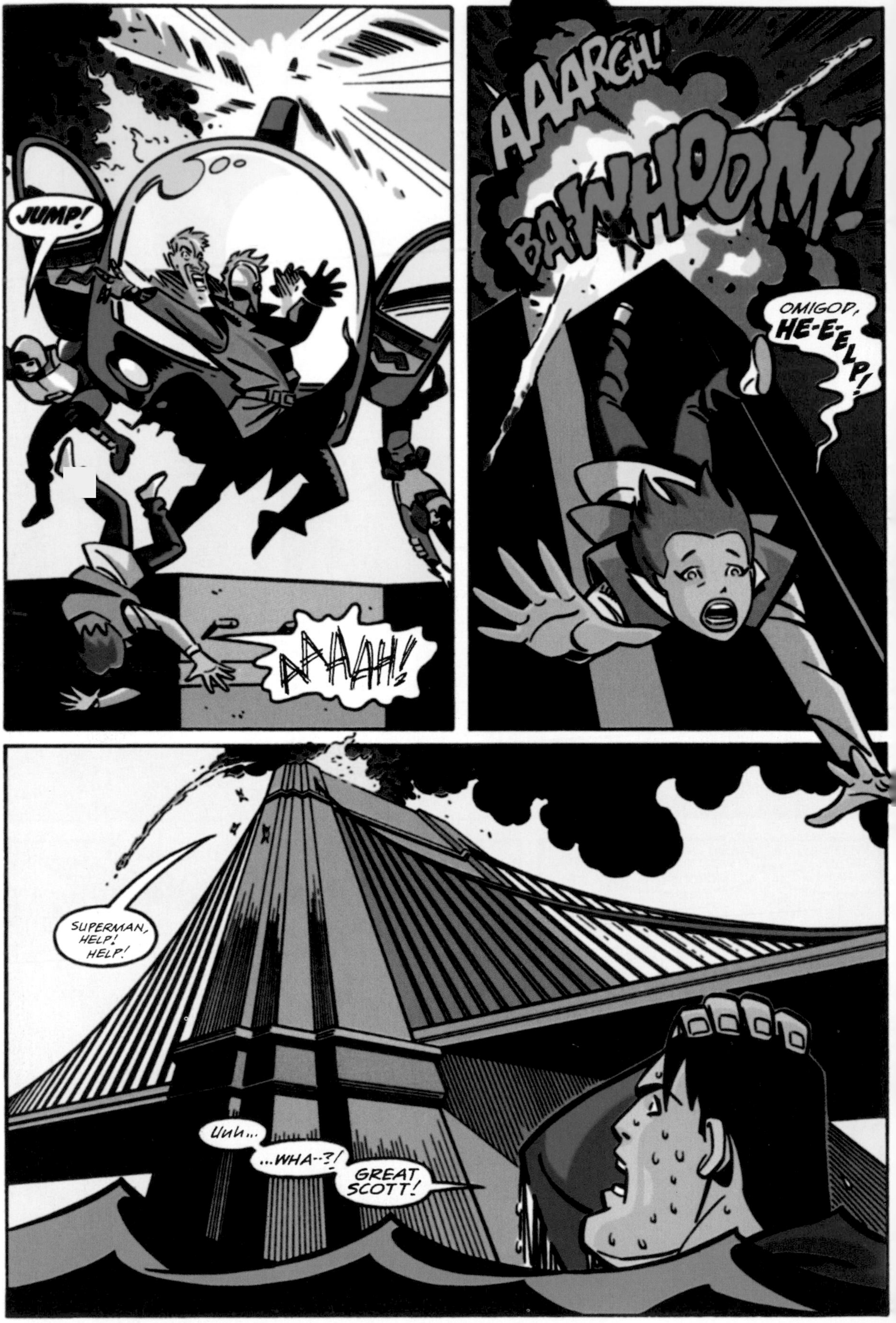
JUMP!
AAAAH!
AAARGH!
BAWHOOM!
OMIGOD, HE-E-ELP!
SUPERMAN, HELP! HELP!
Uuh...
...WHA--?!
GREAT SCOTT!

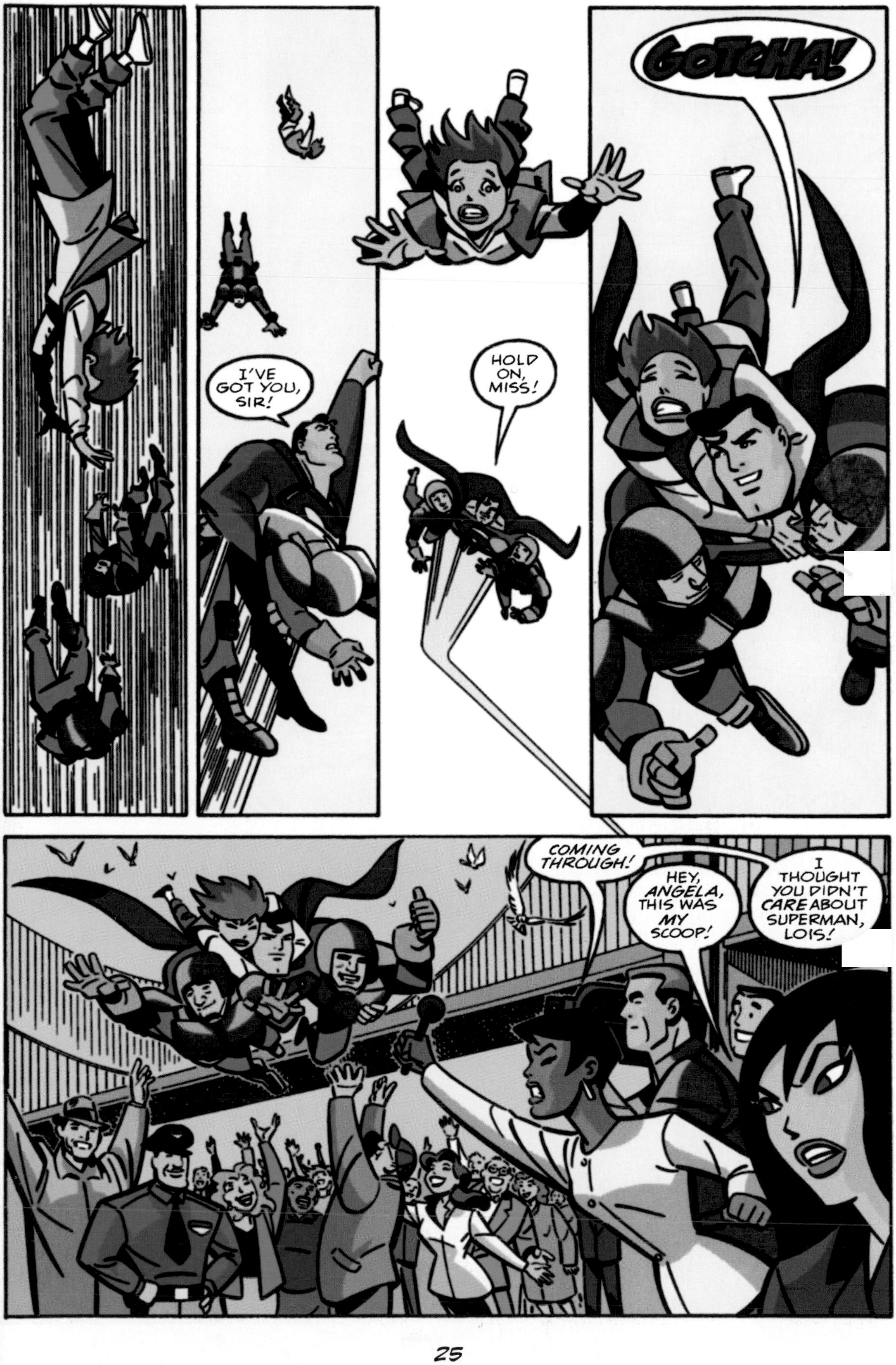
I'VE GOT YOU, SIR!
HOLD ON, MISS!
GOTCHA!
COMING THROUGH!
HEY, ANGELA, THIS WAS MY SCOOP!
I THOUGHT YOU DIDN'T CARE ABOUT SUPERMAN, LOIS!

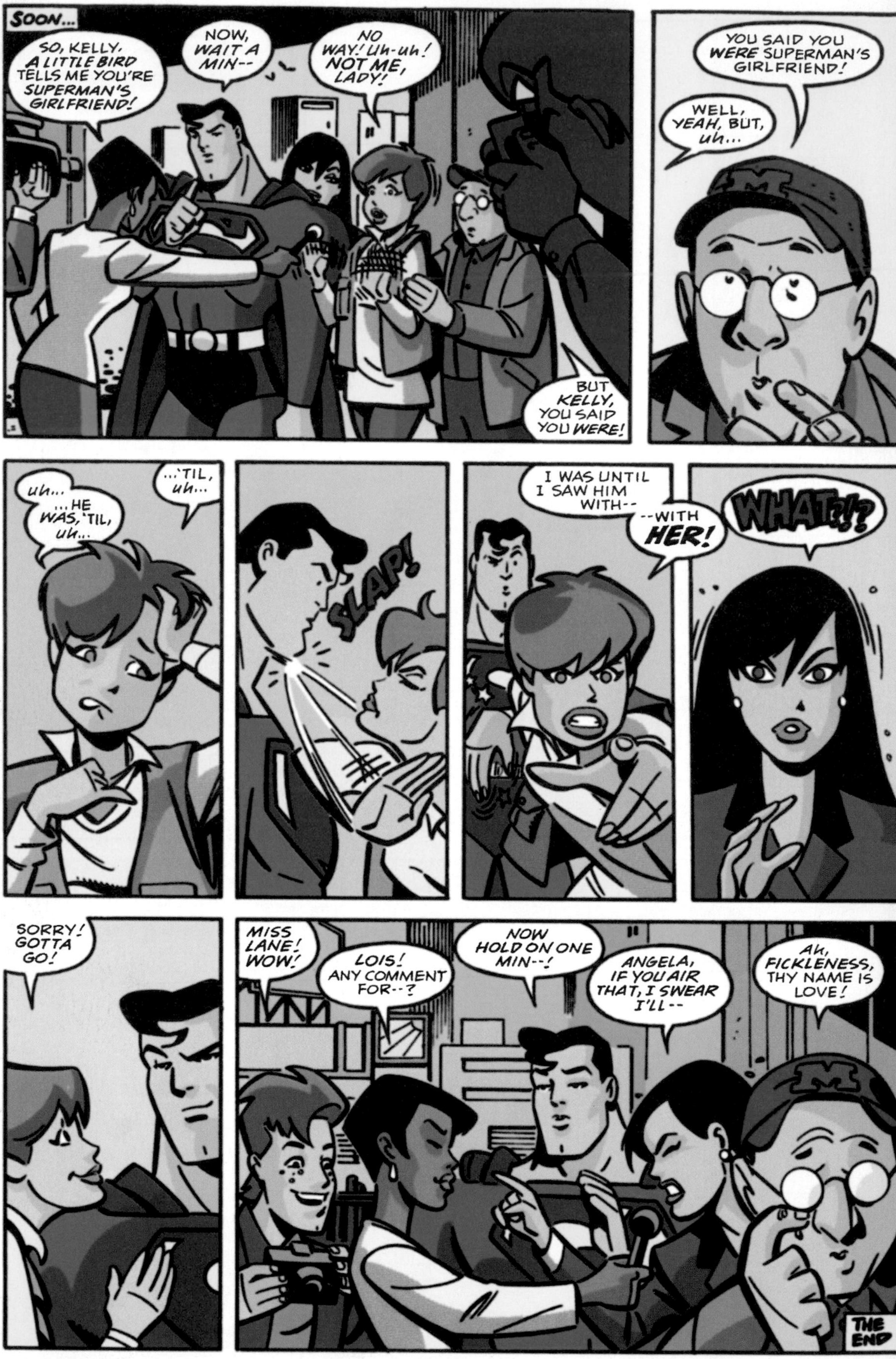
SOON...
SO, KELLY. A LITTLE BIRD TELLS ME YOU'RE SUPERMAN'S GIRLFRIEND!
NOW, WAIT A MIN--
NO WAY! Uh-uh! NOT ME, LADY!
BUT KELLY, YOU SAID YOU WERE!
YOU SAID YOU WERE SUPERMAN'S GIRLFRIEND!
WELL, YEAH, BUT, uh...
uh... ...HE WAS, 'TIL, uh...
...'TIL, uh...
SLAP!
I WAS UNTIL I SAW HIM WITH--
--WITH HER!
WHAT?!?
SORRY! GOTTA GO!
MISS LANE! WOW!
LOIS! ANY COMMENT FOR--?
NOW HOLD ON ONE MIN--!
ANGELA, IF YOU AIR THAT, I SWEAR I'LL--
Ah, FICKLENESS, THY NAME IS LOVE!
THE END

CREATORS

SCOTT McCLOUD WRITER

Scott McCloud is an acclaimed comics creator and author whose best-known work is the graphic novel *Understanding Comics*. His work also includes the science-fiction adventure series *Zot!*, a 12-issue run of *Superman Adventures*, and much more. Scott is the creator of the "24 Hour Comic," and frequently lectures on comics theory.

RICK BURCHETT PENCILLER

Rick Burchett has worked as a comics artist for more than 25 years. He has received the comics industry's Eisner Award three times, Spain's Haxtur Award, and he has been nominated for England's Eagle Award. Rick lives with his wife and two sons near St. Louis, Missouri.

TERRY AUSTIN INKER

Throughout his career, inker Terry Austin has received dozens of awards for his work on high-profile comics for DC Comics and Marvel, such as *The Uncanny X-Men*, *Doctor Strange*, *Justice League America*, *Green Lantern*, and *Superman Adventures.* He lives near Poughkeepsie, New York.

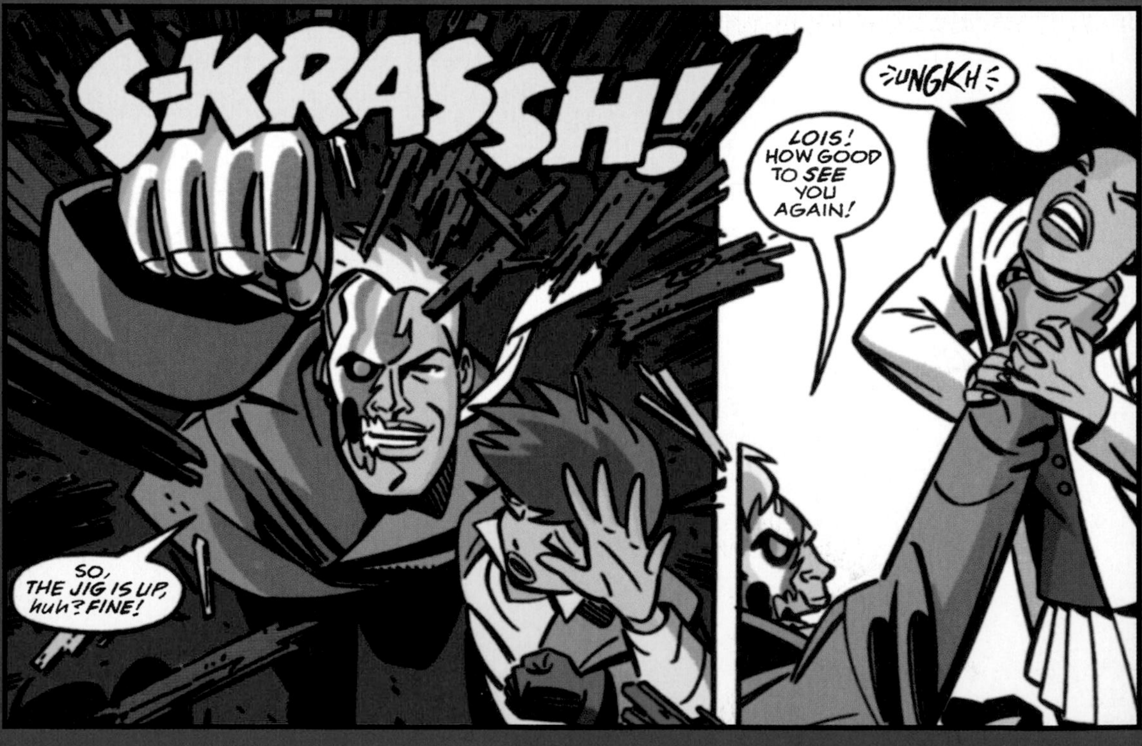
S-KRASSH!
SO, THE JIG IS UP, huh? FINE!
UNGKH
LOIS! HOW GOOD TO SEE YOU AGAIN!

GLOSSARY

alert (uh-LERT)--if you are alert, you pay attention to what is happening and are ready for action

array (uh-RAY)--a large number of things

chivalrous (SHIV-uhl-ruhss)--if someone is chivalrous, they are polite and helpful, especially a man toward a woman

conspiracy (kuhn-SPEER-uh-see)--a secret, illegal plan made by two or more people

evidence (EV-uh-duhnss)--information and facts that help prove something

experience (ek-SPEER-ee-uhnss)--the knowledge and skill you gain by doing something

fickleness (FIK-uhl-ness)--someone who is fickle changes their mind often

hesitates (HEZ-uh-tates)--pauses before doing something

hoax (HOHKS)--a trick or practical joke

scoop (SKOOP)--a big story, or the first report of a story in a news

shady (SHAY-dee)--a shady person is someone who is sneaky or not trustworthy

wharf (WORF)--a long dock, built along a shore, where boats and ships can load and unload

SUPERMAN GLOSSARY

Clark Kent: Superman's alter ego, Clark Kent, is a reporter for the *Daily Planet* newspaper and was raised by Ma and Pa Kent. No one knows he is Superman except for his adopted parents, the Kents.

The Daily Planet: the city of Metropolis's biggest and most read newspaper. Clark, Lois, Jimmy, and Perry all work for the *Daily Planet*.

Invulnerability: Superman's invulnerability makes him impervious to harm. Almost nothing can hurt him -- except for Kryptonite, a radioactive rock from his home planet, Krypton.

Jimmy Olsen: Jimmy is a cub reporter and photographer. He is also a friend to Lois and Clark.

The Kent Family: Ma and Pa Kent found Superman when he crashed to Earth from his home planet, Krypton. They raised him as their own child, giving him the name Clark.

Lex Luthor: Lex believes Superman is a threat to Earth and must be stopped. He will do anything it takes to bring the Man of Steel to his knees.

Lois Lane: like Clark Kent, Lois is a reporter at the *Daily Planet* newspaper. She is also one of Clark's best friends.

Metropolis: the city where Clark Kent (Superman) lives.

Super-strength: one of Superman's most important superpowers is his ability to exert tremendous force using his powerful muscles.

VISUAL QUESTIONS & PROMPTS

1. The title of this comic book is *Be Careful What You Wish For*. Based on this young woman's interactions with the Man of Steel, what do you think the book title means? What did she wish for? How did the experience turn out for her?

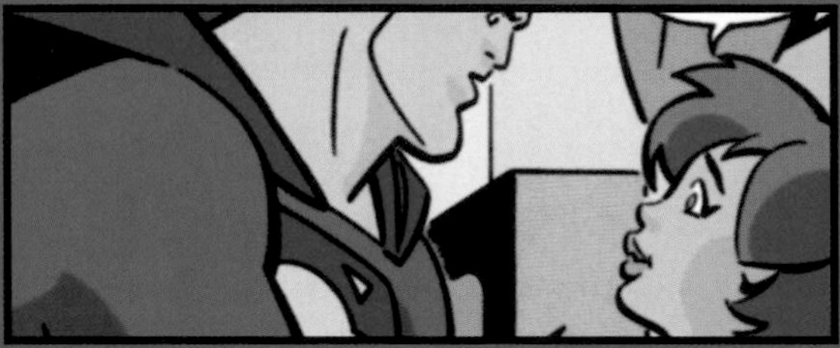

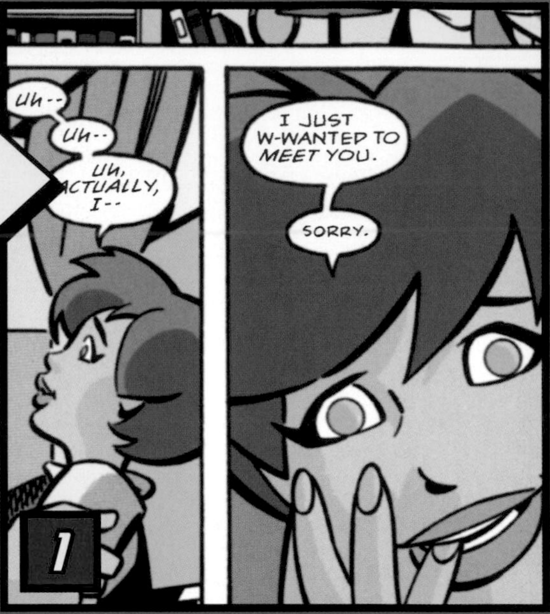
Uh--
Uh--
Uh, ACTUALLY, I--
I JUST W-WANTED TO MEET YOU.
SORRY.
1

2. This single scene of action is broken into three individual panels. Identify what the focus is of each panel. Why do you think the artist decided to break up the scene like this?

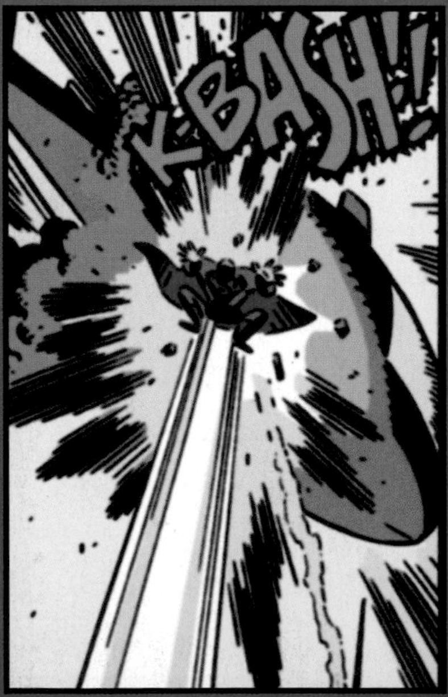
K-BASH!!

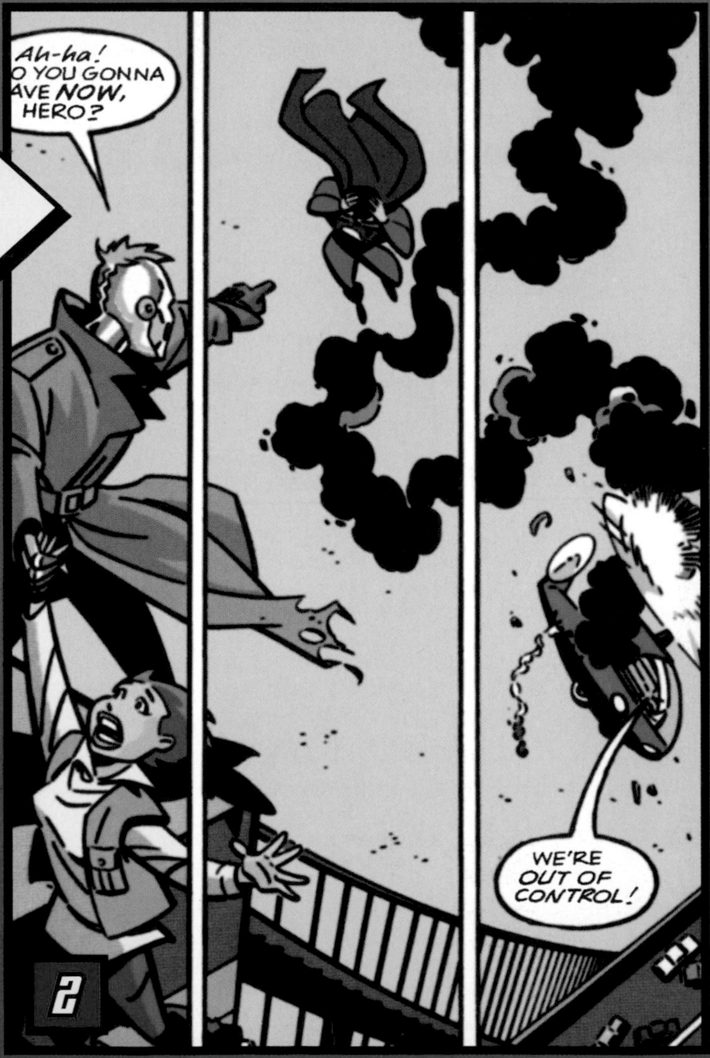
Ah-ha!
O YOU GONNA
AVE NOW,
HERO?
WE'RE OUT OF CONTROL!
2

SUPERMAN ADVENTURES

DC COMICS
SUPERMAN ADVENTURES
MEN OF STEEL
DINI • BURCHETT • AUSTIN

DC COMICS
SUPERMAN ADVENTURES
BE CAREFUL WHAT YOU WISH FOR...

DC COMICS
SUPERMAN ADVENTURES
DISTANT THUNDER

DC COMICS
SUPERMAN ADVENTURES
EYE TO EYE

only from...

STONE ARCH BOOKS™

a capstone imprint www.capstonepub.com

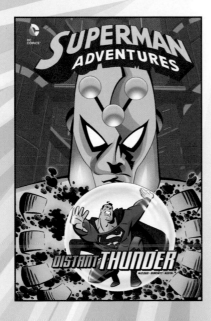

3. Clark Kent is secretly Superman. What kinds of things would make it difficult to be two different people like Clark and the Man of Steel? What advantages and disadvantages are there?

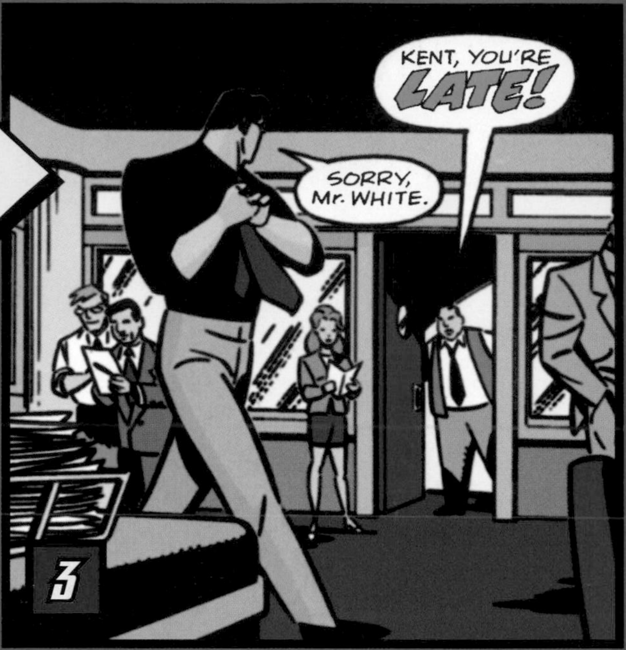
3
KENT, YOU'RE LATE!
SORRY, Mr. WHITE.

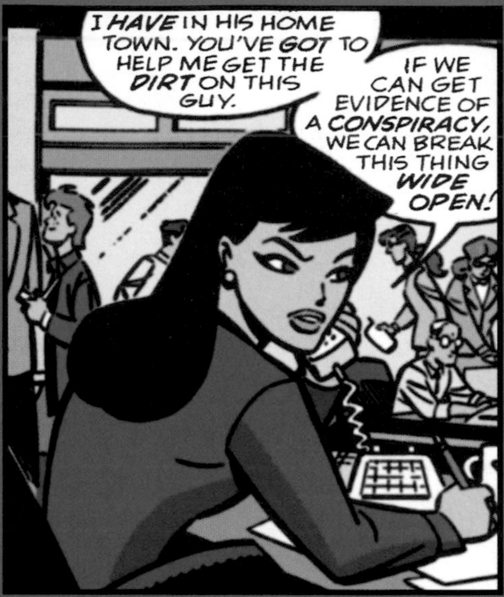
I HAVE IN HIS HOME TOWN. YOU'VE GOT TO HELP ME GET THE DIRT ON THIS GUY.
IF WE CAN GET EVIDENCE OF A CONSPIRACY, WE CAN BREAK THIS THING WIDE OPEN!

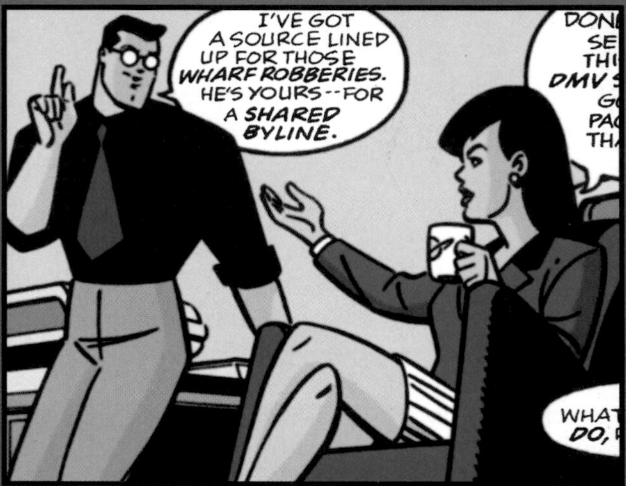
I'VE GOT A SOURCE LINED UP FOR THOSE WHARF ROBBERIES. HE'S YOURS--FOR A SHARED BYLINE.

4. In the panel below, who do you think Clark Kent called? Explain.

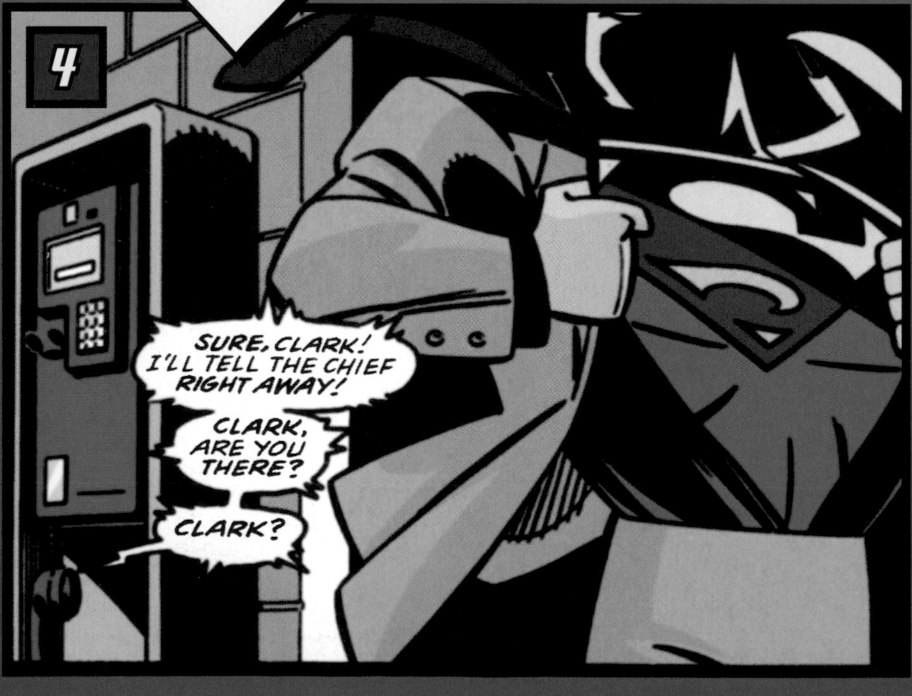
4
SURE, CLARK! I'LL TELL THE CHIEF RIGHT AWAY!
CLARK, ARE YOU THERE?
CLARK?

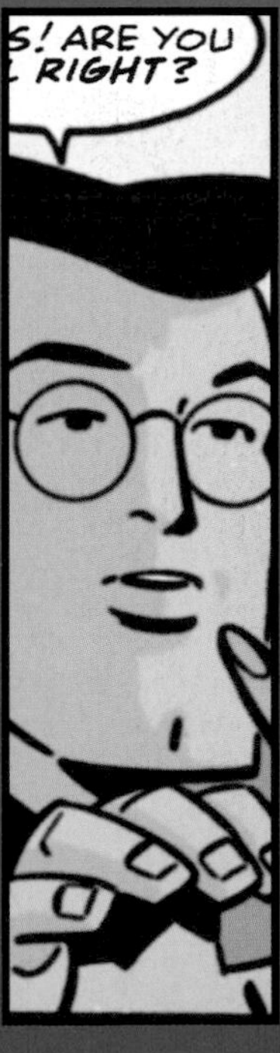